The

Werewolf

Chronicles

The Chosen One

TW HAVENS

Copyright © 2012 by TW Havens

Published by Sarah Book Publishing
(A subsidiary of Litewill Holdings, LLC)

www.sarahbookpublishing.com

85 Industrial Drive
Brownsville, TX 78521

ISBN: **978-1-61456-033-3**

All rights reserved. No part of this publication may be reproduced, stored in a retrieval system or transmitted, in any form, or by any means, electronic, mechanical, recorded, photocopied, or otherwise, without the prior written permission of both the copyright owner and the above-mentioned publisher of this book, except by a reviewer who may quote brief passages in a review.

This is a work of fiction. The characters and events portrayed in this book are a product of the author's imagination or are used fictitiously. Any similarity to real persons, living or dead is purely coincidental and not intended by the author. Some characters and places although real, are only used for historical and geographical reference.

Book Cover Design: Digital Print Shoppe

www.digiprintshoppe.com

Printed in the United States of America

i

I want to dedicate this book to two wonderful people in my life. First is my son Trenton, I love you and will always be there for you. Second, I want to thank the moon of my soul. Thank you for being there for me and helping me through all the hard times. I love you both so much and will always love you.

TW Havens

Chapter I: Secrets Unlocked

The light from the morning sunrise filtered through my bedroom window. I could feel the heat from the sun, and I knew that winter was soon ending. I crawled out of bed slowly, letting my bare feet land on the hardwood floor in my room. I was still half-asleep, and I knew one cure for that - a nice hot shower. As soon as the water started to pour from the spout I started to feel more awake. The heat started to relax my body and help me get ready to start my day. I got out and dressed, putting on my faded jeans and black boots. I was not sure what color shirt to wear today, so I closed my eyes and pointed. As I opened them, I knew it was going to be a white day. I grabbed the white shirt, tossed on my grey hoodie, and headed down the stairs. I found my mom sitting at the table drinking her morning cup of coffee and reading the paper. She was dressed in her black suit, ready to go to work as one of the top realty sales agents in Alaska.

Mom glanced up at me with her blue eyes, giving me a half morning smile and then went back to the paper. I grabbed a plate and tossed some Pop Tarts into the toaster. I poured a glass of orange juice and grabbed my Pop Tarts from the toaster. I sat down at the table with my mom but she got up, grabbed her briefcase, and left. I sat there like usual eating my breakfast in silence.

Mornings have not been the same since my father died last year. He was the glue in the family, he kept us all grounded. My father was the greatest man I have ever known. He was also a hero, not just in my eyes but also in the eyes of the town. He gave his life pulling a little girl from a house on fire. After he died, my mother locked up his office forbidding me from ever entering. I obeyed her for a year, but today I wanted to know why she wanted me to never enter.

I went upstairs and I stood there outside the solid oak door. I wanted to reach for the door handle but something was holding me back. I turned to head back down stairs and then something inside of me snapped. Anger and rage flooded over me, and, in the moment, I turned and kicked the office door in. The door swung back and forth finally stopping halfway closed. I pushed it the rest of the way open and I stood looking into his office. I really did not know what I half expected to find but I hoped I would find him in there. I walked in and found wall-to-wall full of books. In the corner, tucked under the window, was his writing desk made of redwood. My grandfather gave it to him after he published his first book. I slowly walked over to it, scared for some reason but not sure why. Reaching out with my fingers, I let them glide across the top of the desk.

I tried to picture my dad sitting there writing like he used to do. I remember sitting on the floor playing with my Legos as he worked. It was my favorite memory of him; it was the special time we shared together as father and son. I sat down in the antique leather chair he had. I could feel the creases that his body made from being in it so much. In that moment, I felt as if he was still here with me. I decided I'd best fix the door so my mom never knew I disobeyed her. I got up and started to walk over to leave when I tripped over something. I turned and looked behind me to see a plank from the floor popping up.

Great, first the door now the floor, I thought. I got to my feet and walked over to fix the plank when I saw something inside the floor. I bent down lowering my hand into the hole in the floor. When I pulled it out, I realized I was holding something wrapped in a red cloth. I walked back over and sat back down in the chair at the desk and then laid the object covered in cloth on the desk. I looked at it for a moment, not sure if I should unwrap it or not. Being the curious sixteen years old I was, well, let's say I had to do it.

I slowly removed the cloth to find a brown leather-bound book. It looked to me to be a journal of some kind. I untied the leather strings that kept the journal closed. I opened it to the first page, was shocked at what I saw. "This journal belongs to Elijah M Blackmane." I knew that name, it sounded familiar to me for some reason. I turned to the first page of the journal.

"March 26th 1876"

"I started this journal to keep track of my new life. Ever since my seventeenth birthday, my life was turned upside down. The night of my birthday, I started to run a fever. It was bad and my

2

mother and father did not know how to break it. I went through the night fighting the delusions of the fever and the pain I felt all over my body. When morning came it was weird, the fever was gone and the pain no longer existed. I felt refreshed, energized as if I could do anything. My mother did not want me going out and helping with the morning chores. However, I could not leave my father to attend to the ranch duties alone. I went out and started on the back pasture fixing the fence posts that were rotted away. After that, my dad asked me to help feed the animals. This was when I started to notice things. I went out to the barn and when I started to open the barn doors, the horses started to go crazy.

I entered to find my own horse, Moonstar, going crazy as I got near her. She was kicking and trying to break out of the stables. I dropped the pail of apples and ran out of the barn not sure what was going on. I decided to spend the rest of the day away from the animals. The sun started to set and mom called father and I to come eat dinner. It was dad's favorite, meat and potatoes stew with bread rolls. I finished dinner and went outside. I noticed the moon was starting to become full. As I looked up at the moon, I felt like I was in some kind of trance. I could not pull my gaze from the moon; it was as if it was calling to me. Then I felt something. My eyes felt as if they were straining. I turned to look at the mirror hanging next to the lantern; what I saw scared me.

My eyes were no longer hazel but yellow and the white was now black. I backed away slowly looking around. I started to rub my eyes hoping it would make them go back to normal, but that was false hope. A pain started to shoot through my body. I yelled in agony. Dropping to my knees, I heard the front door open and my mom calling to me. I wanted to turn away from her, but I was on all fours looking up at her with my new eyes. I could smell the fear washing over her. She put her hands to her mouth trying to not scream. She started to back away, inching towards the door.

My body started to twist and turn in an unnatural way. My bones were breaking and my muscles were shifting. I heard my father come out but I could not see him. My clothes started to rip and tear until my body was no longer human. I was now something else, a monster, a massive black wolf. I looked my parents in the eyes. I wanted to run away and hide but I was no longer in control.

I could not stop as my new beast ripped into my parents killing them. I watched it all happen - unable to do anything about it.

Soon it was as if I was gone, just faded away. The beast now had complete control over me. I had no idea what he did the whole night. I just remember waking up next to the stream on the Collin's lands. My body was covered in blood and I found that I also killed the Collins. I found the bodies lying across the land one after another."

I closed the journal, lost at everything I just read. Was this real? I asked myself. It can't be possible. I grabbed the journal and left, out of my father's office. I headed to my room and jumped on my bed to continue to *read the journal.*

"April 7ᵗʰ 1876"

"It has been weeks since I shifted into the beast that killed my family. I was still not sure what was going on with me. I decided to travel to the local tribe here and try to talk to the shaman, I remember my father had trading relations with them. I had to travel on foot so it took me a week to reach them since no horse would let me near them. Before I even entered into the tribe's lands, I was met by the elder shaman. It was as if he knew I was coming. He stood there in his skins, his hands raised as if telling me to stop. It was snowing outside but I was not even near being cold. Since I shifted my body has been running hot, my senses and strength and speed all heightened. The shaman looked at me chanting. I felt something like an energy coming from the shaman.

Before I knew it, I felt something flowing into me through my mouth, a blue energy coming from the Shaman. 'Welcome, child of the moon, to the tribal lands of the Abunaki.'

I was stunned; whatever it was that he did made it possible for me to understand his speech. 'How can I understand you?' I asked him, touching my throat.

The Shaman laughed. 'It is because I allow you to… now tell me what brings you to our lands?'

I was still shocked at what he did. 'You called me a child of the moon! What does that mean?'

The Shaman walked over and took a seat on a small boulder next to the creek. 'It started when the Great Spirit fell from the moon. She was the great creator of the wolves. She herself took the form of a wolf. The story goes; One day the Great Spirit was hunting in the forest of the Blackwood when she found a young hunter. She watched him hidden from his sight. She found him to be beautiful to her. So the Great Spirit took the form of a beautiful young lady and seduced the young hunter. The Spirit left the hunter while he slept, shifting back into her wolf form. Soon she found herself pregnant. Months passed, and she gave birth to five pups. The pups were the first of the children of the moon to be born. They grew to be able to shift from wolf to man when the moon was full. Through them, they started to mate with the human population and that is how the werewolf was born.'

I looked at the Shaman not scared but I finally understand what I was. 'So my family's bloodline must be directly descended from one of the original children of the Great Spirit?' I asked the Shaman.

He stood up, picking up a broken branch and tossing it into the creek. 'That is true but I have met both your mother and your father and they do not carry the magical essence of a child of the moon.'

I just looked at him my face losing all impressions. 'What do you mean? How is it that I am one of the children of the moon than?' I asked with rage in my voice.

The Shaman walked over and placed his hand on my shoulder looking me in the eyes. 'That answer I cannot give you, but I can help you. Travel south until you come to mountains as green as the grass you stand on. There you will find other children of the moon, they can help you uncover the answer you search for.' Before I could say anything he disappeared like a ghost who was not there."

I turned to look and I noticed that it was no longer morning and I spent the majority of the day reading this journal. I knew I should take a break but there was something about the journal that had me.

"June 17th 1876"

"I did not leave right away. I spent the next month trying to sell my family's land and get past the full moon before I travelled. Winter was gone, summer had come, and the snow melted away. I sold my family's home to a local farmer. He gave me 1000 dollars and a horse that ran away from me the next day. I travelled south as the Shaman told me to. I found myself deep in a green forest with trees that reached for the heavens. It was a beautiful and enchanting place. I walked through the forest taking in the sounds and new sights around me. Then something caught my nose, a scent I had never smelled before, but it smelled so familiar to me. I followed it using my newfound sense of smell. I soon found myself standing outside a fort. The giant wood gate protected the people inside from the dangers outside in the forest.

'Who goes there?' I heard a voice call to me. I looked up to see a young man about my age standing on the wall holding a gun. It was pointed at me and he looked like he knew how to use it.

'My name is Elijah Blackmane. I am just looking for a place to rest. I have money, I can pay,' I yelled to him.

He turned his head looking behind him, and then turned back to me. 'You may enter!' As he said that, the giant gated door opened and I saw woman and children scrambling around to get away from me. I looked around, and then found myself in the company of a man.

He had long, black hair and blue eyes, his outfit looked simple made of black and grey colors. 'Welcome to Fort Wilderness. I am Hannibal, and I am the controller of the fort. What is your name sir?' he asked me with a half-smile

I looked at him and I could sense he was like me but not like me. He smelled of hatred and rage. I felt it was me who made him feel this way. I also felt a powerful energy coming from him.

6

'I am Elijah Blackmane. I have travelled from the farthest part of the north,' I said to him.

'Well, that is quite a ways to travel! What brings you this far south?'

I started to become enraged, I felt him pushing at me and my inner wolf did not like it. I looked him in his eyes and something compelled me to not let my gaze drop. He looked back at me, and then, for some reason, he dropped his gaze and I felt my dominance over him.

'I am in search of something. Can you show me where I can rest? I have been travelling for a long time.'

Hannibal looked at me, and then turned waving for me to follow. I walked slowly behind him, looking around and taking in the territory. I noticed that the only animals in the fort were pigs and sheep and they stayed far away from us. We stopped outside a little rundown cabin. It had a small bed in it. It was not much but I would make do. I entered and Hannibal left me alone to become acclimated with the cabin. I set my pack on the ground taking off my coat and lying in bed. It did not take long for me to fall asleep. I was exhausted and needed to rest. I do not know how long I was sleep but I awoke to a knock coming on my door. I climbed out of bed and then walked over to open the door. Standing outside was a teenage boy who had on only a pair of pants.

'I need you to come with me. The moon is rising and we cannot stay in the fort at night,' he said to me with a tremble in his voice.

I looked at him, then his scent hit my nose, and yes - he was like me. I took off the majority of my cloths except for my pants. He started to run, and I followed behind him. We exited out the main gate. The guard closed it behind us. I followed him, we were moving with great speed, getting as far as we could away from the fort. We arrived at a waterfall that was nestled deep in the forest far away from the fort. I stopped to see about six others including Hannibal waiting for us. He stood atop a giant boulder as if he was the king of the world. I looked at the others. As they bowed to him, I turned back to look at Hannibal. I felt a vibration of energy

7

coming from Hannibal. I knew he dominated over the wolves here. He was the alpha of this pack. The wind started to pick up, and the trees creaked at the wind. I felt another pull. I looked up at the moon. She was calling to me.

I felt the heat in my body start to rise. The shift was coming. I felt my eyes changing. I looked around to see the pack was already in transition. I was still a new werewolf, so my change took longer, and it was a new experience for me. This is the first time I have seen the change through my eyes. The pain started to take hold of me. I could not remain standing. It once again brought me to my knees digging my hands into the muddy ground. Every time my wolf comes out, the shift gets a little bit easier. I looked up and noticed that they were done and waiting on me. I looked up to where Hannibal was, and now I saw a massive red wolf. The pain started to fade away and in that moment I was done, the shift was completed. I stood, the only black wolf of the pack. I was the same size as Hannibal, but the rest of the pack was a bit smaller than we were.

Hannibal turned his newly formed wolf head to the sky letting out a long howl. The other wolves cocked their heads to his howl and started to howl with him. I watched trying to take this all in learning everything I could from them. The howling stopped, Hannibal took off, and the pack followed. I started to follow behind them. That was when the hunt was on and my wolf took over. Again, I was no longer in control. I faded away, waiting to see the damage my wolf brother would cause on this night. Just like every other full moon, I awoke the next morning covered in blood. But I was back at the waterfall. The rest of the pack was in the waterfall washing. I looked around but there were no bodies anywhere in sight, this was strange.

I washed off using the water from the falls and then I felt a hand on my shoulder. I turned to find Hannibal still naked looking down at me. 'You are brand new, aren't you, boy?' he said to me. I hated that he could tell, but it was the truth.

'So what if I am? What does it matter?' I asked him with rage in my voice.

Hannibal backed up a foot from me. 'Calm down, kid, I know because you still have not learned to be the one in charge instead of your wolf. I had to work hard to control mine, as he was not easy to watch out for. When the pack and I shift, we are in complete control, not our wolves. We do not kill humans, not anymore.'

I looked at him. How did he learn to control his wolf? I wondered. 'How did you do it? Learn to control the wolf in you?' I said standing up and putting my pants back on.

'When you look at me, how old do you think I am?' he said with a laugh.

'I do not know, forty?' I said to him. He turned, and the rest of the pack started to laugh with him. 'I am over two hundred years old. I am not the oldest. There are others out there who are thousands of years old. You stop aging the day you trigger the curse!'

I looked at him trying to get around that age he claimed to be. 'I did not trigger anything. I changed on the night of my eighteenth birthday.'

Hannibal turned to look at me. I could soon smell fear on him. 'You were not killed in a violent way? You changed once you reached a certain age?' I nodded, agreeing with what he said.

'I need to know who your father is,' Hannibal asked me with a demanding tone.

'I do not know. I travelled out here to find out that very question,' I replied to him.

Hannibal looked to his pack. They all left, leaving just him and me at the waterfall. 'I met a wolf once over a hundred years ago. He looked to be young like you but he was very powerful and very old. He, like you, did not need to die to trigger his bloodline. He told me once he turned twenty, his wolf awoke. His name was Balthazar and he was the one who taught me how to control my wolf. After he left, I stayed here making this my territory. I built the

9

fort for our kind. A sanctuary for them to come and not have to worry about killing any more humans.'

I soon realized I was wrong about Hannibal. He was not the monster I thought he was going to be. 'Does everyone in the fort know about us?' I asked him.

Hannibal looked at me, 'Yes, they do know. We protect them. A few years ago, three rogue wolves came into this territory and tried to kill. My pack and I stepped in. We have sworn to forever protect those from any supernatural threat that comes here. I will allow you to stay long enough to learn to control your wolf. But after that, I need you to leave. You are like me. We are born alphas, not born to follow, but born to lead. I cannot allow a dominant wolf like you to stay in my pack!' he said as he started back to the fort.

I turned my head to the sound of my mom's car coming up the drive looking over at the clock I noticed it was already 6:00 PM. I spent the whole day reading this journal lost in the enchantment of it. I tucked the journal into my nightstand. I got up and ran down the stairs grabbing a frozen pizza and tossing it in the oven. When mom worked passed 5:00 PM I was responsible for dinner. The front door opened and closed I heard my mom walk across the hardwood floors in her heels. The tapping of the shoe would make it impossible for her to ever sneak in. "Welcome home, mom…how was your day?" I yelled to her. But she did not respond as she started up the stairs. That is when I remembered not fixing my dad's office door.

I quickly started to run up the stairs - but it was too late. I found my mom looking into my father's office. She turned and looked at me. I could see the rage building in her. I knew I was in real trouble this time. "What the hell, Liam? I told you not to ever go in here. I wanted to go through the office before you had a chance to go in. This house we live in was in your family for over four generations, and you decided to break a hand-carved door. You grandfather carved that door and put it in here. What were you thinking?"

10

I looked at her. I could see sadness coming from her, too. I started to feel bad about what I did. I did not want to make my mother sad. It has been a year since my father died, and I hoped Mom would have gotten passed Dad's death a tiny bit. But, by her reaction, I could tell she was not even close to being on the road to recovery.

I walked over and took my mom's tiny little body into my arms, trying to help sooth her sadness. I started to hear her crying into my chest. Then she pushed me away and looked up at me. "Clean this up now and fix the fucking door, Liam!" she said turning and heading to her room. I went down stairs pulling the overcooked pizza from the over.

While talking to my mom it burnt and dinner was officially ruined. I tossed the pizza in the trashcan and went back up the stairs to fix the door. It took me a few hours but I finally got it fixed. I closed the door to find my mom watching me in the hallway. She looked tired and run down. I heard her crying in her room the whole time I was working on the door. Her red hair was in a tattered mess, her makeup smeared on her face. "Mom, why don't you go take a shower and relax? I'll go into town and get you some dinner. I kind of burnt the pizza."

She nodded, turned, and went back into her room. I grabbed my keys from my dresser and headed out. I climbed into my jeep and started to head into town, the drive was nice but I could not stop thinking about the journal. I stopped in at Harry's burgers and grabbed a few burgers and fries. I also got my mom a strawberry milkshake, she loved them. I headed back home taking a bit longer to get home than getting to town.

The road had a dead deer in it, so I had to slowly go around it. I pulled up to the house and entered to find my mom sitting on the couch. In her hand, she had the journal. I looked at her and she glared back at me. "Your father always hoped the werewolf gene would skip you like it did him. He did not want you to have to go through it. This journal belonged to your great grandfather. He lived a very long time. He died in World War II; he was burned to death like your father was in the fire. The only way to kill a werewolf is either by fire or decapitation. Your birthday is next

11

week, and I am so scared for you. I love you, Liam, and you are all I have left."

I walked over and set the burgers on the table handing my mom her milkshake. She took it from me with a smile. I felt better seeing her smile. I walked over, kissed my mom on her forehead, and went up to my room. I closed my door and the thought of becoming a werewolf started to weigh heavily on my shoulders. I was scared but I was also very intrigued by the idea of gaining all that power. I heard my mom coming up the stairs stopping in front of my door.

"Liam, are you okay?" she said to me through the door.

"Yeah, mom, I'm good. No worries," I replied to her. I watched her shadow move away from my door. I opened the door to find the journal sitting by my door. I grabbed it and closed my door taking my position back on the bed. I opened the journal back up, picking up where I left off.

"October 9th 1876"

"It has been a few months since I came to the fort hidden away in the forest. Little by little, I am learning to control my wolf. Hannibal said I am learning unnaturally fast. Tonight is the full moon and I am ready to be in control during the run. Since coming here, I have grown to respect Hannibal and follow his words or wisdom he gives out. We all sat down in the dining hall in the main building for dinner. Eating before shifting helps with the change. The energy helps push it along faster. We all sat as a pack, as a family. I have come to care about the pack members, even looking after them. I still butt heads with Hannibal because we are both dominant wolves.

We finished dinner and the moon started to rise, which meant we needed to head out. We all met up at the waterfall like every other full moon. I was usually the last one to arrive. I got there, stripped off my pants, and got ready for the change. Hannibal was of course standing on the usual boulder looking down on us. That was something that I hated. My wolf also grew angry and enraged at the sight of Hannibal looking down on us.

The full moon started to peak, the light of the moon shot down on us filling us with great energy. Basking in the moonlight was one of the high points of shifting. The energy we feel from the moon is intoxicating to us, happiness takes us over. The shift started to happen, beginning with our eyes, but this time the pain was not as bad. I shifted just as fast as the others did. Soon we no longer stood as men, but as massive wolves. This time I was the one in control; I no longer obeyed the wolf inside me. We took off and the power that I felt was amazing. I was running at a great speed keeping up with Hannibal with ease. We spent the good part of the evening just running and exploring the forest. We soon came upon a group of deer and the thought of the hunt enthralled us. Hannibal howled startling the deer giving us something to chase. Hannibal took off after the buck, the leader of the deer, and I followed. I knew it was going to cause an issue. But I could feel my wolf; he wanted to taste the flesh of the powerful buck. I was soon running neck and neck with Hannibal. He turned and looked at me, growling as we ran. I looked at him, and then took off leaving him with my tail in his face. I used my speed and strength bringing the buck to the ground, my mouth crushing its throat.

I snapped it with great ease. I turned to see Hannibal looking at me. I could feel his rage as he watched me, but I won and I was the more dominate of us. He would not dare try to attack me, for he knew I would win the fight. I fed on the buck enjoying the kill, and enjoying the way Hannibal was acting. I let go of the kill and walked away from the buck. I turned and saw Hannibal clawing and eating my leftovers. I knew in that moment that my time here with this pack was over, and it was time for me to move on. I left the pack that night and did not look back. I headed back to the north to build my own life. I know now that I was not cursed, but more blessed being given this power I have.

I took more time traveling back north than I did coming here. I enjoyed the views of the different lands as I travelled. I even stopped in some small towns and took in the company of a woman from time to time. I arrived back home to find my old home abandoned. Which I did not expect to find. I wonder what happened to the family I sold it too. I looked around and found three tombs in the back. It was the family that bought my house and lands. I decided since they had died, I would retake my home for mine. I tore down the old shack I lived in with my parents to build a much bigger and nicer home."

I looked over at the clock, it was nearly midnight and I needed to get some sleep for school tomorrow. I placed the journal on my nightstand and got into bed. It did not take long for me to fall asleep. I soon found myself dreaming, and in my dream, I was in the company of Elijah. He stood before me in what looked like a cowboy outfit. I could see his lips moving but I could not hear what he was saying. I woke to find myself on the floor next to my bed. I was not sure how I got there. I pulled myself off the floor and looked at the clock it was 6:00 AM and time to get ready for school. I took a quick shower, putting on the same clothes from the day before and then headed down stairs.

I found my mom once again sitting, drinking her coffee. This time she closed her newspaper and looked at me. "We need to talk, Liam," she said smiling at me. I poured some orange juice and then took a seat at the table.

"What is it we need to talk about mom?" I asked taking a drink of my orange juice.

"On your birthday this Friday, I want you to stay home until we know if it passed you or not. If it does, I will make your birthday up to you. It will be safer this way until we know exactly what is going to happen."

I looked at her rolling my eyes, I hated that she was acting like this. I got up from the table and poured out what was left of my orange juice. I turned and looked at my mom "Whatever you want mom!" I said as I grabbed my backpack and left the house. I pulled up to the student parking lot to find my two best friends, Mark and Robert, waiting for me at my usual parking spot. Mark was a bigger guy built like a two-ton truck with short red hair. As for Robert, he was your run of a mill computer geek with suspenders and pocket protector. His long black hair was always blocking his face. I parked my jeep and grabbed my pack getting out. "Hey, Liam, it's about time you got here!" Robert said walking over to me. We went to morning class and the school day ran just as usual

14

as always. During 6th period, I was no longer with Robert and Mark. They had different classes. I hated 6th period, it was history class and Mr. Warren was a crazy old man. It's two days until my birthday, but it's also two days to graduation. I am almost done living the high school dream.

Chapter II: Summer Moon

The day has finally arrived! I am eighteen on this day. I stood here looking at myself in my green gown, all ready to walk the stage later. I was both excited and very nervous, still not sure what is going to happen tonight. My mom was out working, but she promised to meet me at my graduation at the school. I had an hour to kill before I needed to get to the school so, I decided to read a little more of the journal.

"January 10th 1943"

"In the last sixty-six years I have seen so much change. Horses went out when the automobile was created. I cannot say I am heartbroken about that since animals hated me. Now I can stop walking so much and drive where I need to go. It was a bit difficult getting used to the new age of electricity and technology. These days, in order to live, you need to have a job, but I was lucky my land was an oil field. The oil became my life, giving me a near endless supply of money. I moved from my family's lands to a small town in Alaska called Wasilla. I picked this town because it was small and I would be able to hide away here. Being a werewolf, I stayed eternally young so I needed a place I could be left alone. I built a modest three-bedroom, two-bath log cabin home. Spending most of my time to myself - that is, until I met Cece. She was a waitress at the local diner. She has the most beautiful light blue eyes I had ever seen. Her hair is like long locks of gold running down her back.

After I met her the first time, I could not stay away. I made it a point to go into town twice a week just so I could see her. For a month, I followed this routine ordering the same thing every time. I finally got the nerve to ask her if she would like to get some coffee sometime. I waited until her shift was over, standing outside next to my motorcycle. I watched her as she turned off all the lights and locked up. She started to walk towards her pickup truck when another truck pulled up next to hers. I stood my ground just watching, but my wolf was going nuts - he knew something was up.

A tall man got out of the truck. He was built like a wrestler or something. I watched as he walked up to her and she turned

16

shaking her head. I watched for a minute while he yelled at her, but then he did something I could not ignore. He struck her, knocking her to ground, and in that moment, I walked over stepping between them.

'Cece, who the fuck is this?' The man asked her.

She looked up at me. 'Boris, he is just a regular. Do not hurt him,' she said with a trembling voice.

'If I was you, I would turn around and get back into your truck and leave!' I said to Boris with a bit of power in my voice.

Boris looked at me with his brown eyes and started to laugh. 'Cece, this is sweet. You have a protector... but I am sorry I am going to have to kick his ass!' Boris raised his fist back.

I knew he was going to try. His arm shot at me, his fist guided towards my face. I let him connect the punch. 'Mother Fucker,' Boris yelled grabbing his fist. Being a werewolf meant that I was built like steel. His fist broke upon impact with the side of my face. I grabbed Boris by his neck lifting him off the ground making his feet dangle.

'Get into your truck and do not ever come back here again. If you do, next time you will not walk away!' I said to him with a growl. I tossed him against his truck door. He fell to the ground and quickly got up into his truck and took off. I turned around, offering my hand to help her up. As Cece looked up at me, I could see the tears in her eyes.

She jumped up off the ground hugging me, burrowing her face into my neck. I was lost; in all my years I had never had any women warm up to me. I closed my arms around her whispering into her ears, 'I promise I will always be here for you.'

She started to slow her breathing and the crying started to become less and less. She started to release her grip on me pulling away. I did not want to let her go but I knew I had to. After that day, Cece and I soon started to grow more and more in love. She was the one. I knew it and so did my wolf, we had found our mate.

17

Cece quit her job and moved in with me. We were married soon after and she became pregnant with my son, Nolan."

My alarm clock went off and I looked over to see I had just less than twenty minutes to get to school. But I started to think maybe I should not attend and just stay home in case the wolf gene did not skip me. I called my mom, but she did not answer so I left her a message letting her know I would be home. I stood looking around knowing that Elijah lived in this very house, which was a bit weird for me. I grabbed the journal and headed down stairs sitting in the giant sofa in the corner of the living room.

"June 25th 1944"

"I left Cece and Nolan to go and fight the Nazi's. I wanted to protect what was mine. I became a Captain and shipped off to a small army base in northern Italy. I found Italy to be a bit unsettling, nothing familiar about it at all."

I looked at the entry trying to figure out why it cut off where it did. Then I remembered that he died over there. I set the journal on the in table and looked out the window. The thermometer that hung out my window read 87 degrees. I could see the sun starting to set and my stomach started to become twisted with knots. I knew even if I was destined to be one of the children of the moon I would not shift until next full moon. I found myself dozing off in the comfy chair I was sitting in. When I awoke, I noticed my mother was not home yet. I started to climb out of the chair when I started to feel drowsy. I sat back down. I was not sure what was wrong, and then I started to burn up and I knew what was wrong. The werewolf gene did not skip me and I was starting the change. A part of me was excited but another part was terrified.

The fever was too much and it caused me to pass out in the chair. The sound of my mom's car pulling up awoke me. I did not want to worry her so I climbed out of the chair slowly trying to make it to my room before she came in. I found myself climbing up the stairs as massive pain shot up my back and I screamed in agony. The door to the house flew open and my mom looked at me.

"Oh… dear god, no, please, not you!" she said running over to help me up the stairs. She let go of me as fast as she grabbed me. My skin was so hot it made her let go, she just cried watching me climb up the steps. I reached up grabbing the rail to try and pull myself to my feet. But it was no use. My mom was soon by my side again wearing oven mitts. She pulled me up, helping me to my room.

I climbed into bed sweating. My mom grabbed the fan from my closet plugging it in next to the bed. She turned it on pointing it towards me to help cool me down then she was gone. I lay there looking up at the glow in the dark stars that my dad put up for me when I was five. I heard my door open, and my mom stood there looking at me. "Please, come quickly!" I was lost, I thought she was talking to me but she was on the phone.

About fifteen minutes passed, and there was a knock at the door. "WE ARE UP HERE!" my mom yelled from atop the stairs. I could not move but I heard soft footsteps climbing the stairs. My bedroom door pushed open more, and to my surprise, my mom's friend Sage walked in.

She had brown eyes, caramel coloring to her skin, and her hair was cut to her shoulders curled at the ends with the color of coal. Sage walked over to my bed placing her hand on my forehead. Like my mom, she quickly pulled away, and her gaze went to my mom. "He is too far into the change for me to stop it. If I tried, there would be a chance it would kill him!" she said to my mom. I looked at Sage. Her eyes turned to me and she smiled.

"Do not worry, Liam, you will be just fine. By tomorrow, you will be feeling right as rain." Her southern accent was beautiful. She left my side, grabbing my mom and pulling her out of the room. I tried to listen in, but it was as if my ears were plugged. I felt a coolness sweep over my body as the fever started to lower.

I decided to try and get some sleep. I slowly rolled over on my side, trying to move with the pain. It helped. I soon started to close my eyes and go to sleep. The night went by fast. When I woke up, I found my mom sleeping next to my bed in a chair she brought in. I did not want to wake her, so I climbed out of bed trying to be as

19

quite as a cat stalking its prey. I stretched, not making a sound. I felt better, actually I felt better than I ever had before.

I remember reading about this part, the new energy I had inside of me. There was something else I felt, as if there was something inside of me. A presence that was talking to me but it was so faint, it was a whisper. I walked down the stairs making my way to the kitchen to pour my morning glass of orange juice. As I drank my orange juice, I started to think about tonight. It was a full moon and I would change. I do not want to harm my mother like Elijah did his parents.

I walked down the hall heading to the bathroom when I stopped. I looked over at the bookcase in the hallway and I could swear I could feel air coming from it. I put my ear closer to it, and sure enough, I could hear the air like a leak in a tire. I started to search the bookcase for anything that would open it. My hand ran over a groove on the side of the outline. I pushed it and the bookcase opened a bit. I grabbed it pulling it open enough to see a stairwell leading down. I had always wondered if there was some kind of cellar for the house.

Following the stairs, I came to a metal door. I opened it to find a room with cement walls and a cell like you would find in a jail. It hit me then. This must have been were Elijah locked himself up at. Then I started to think. In his journal he said he gained control over the wolf inside of him. Why would he need this room? I turned and then went back up the stairs, leaving the room and locking the bookcase back up. I decided since I was up I should make some breakfast for my mom and I. "LIAM!" I heard my mom yell. I turned the corner standing at the bottom of the stairs.

"I'm down here, mom, in the kitchen!" I yelled back at her. I went back to the kitchen and heard my mom coming down the stairs. She turned the corner and I have to say she looked pretty tore up. I could tell she did not sleep well. "Mom sit down breakfast is almost ready," I said to her, pouring her morning coffee and handing it to her.

As she looked at me I could see worry and concern in her eyes. "How are you feeling?" she asked me with a soft voice.

"I am just fine, mom, don't worry. I want you to go stay somewhere else tonight. It's a full moon and I don't want to hurt you," I said to her handing her a plate with eggs, potatoes and bacon on it.

"After breakfast, Liam, I want to show you something."

We sat eating what I had made for breakfast. I was not really hungry, so I picked at my plate mostly. As for my mom, well, she finished her breakfast and then got up placing our plates in the sink. "Follow me," she said, leaving the kitchen and heading down the hallway that lead to the downstairs bathroom. She stopped in front of the bookcase, pushing the button making it open again. I followed her down into the room with the cell in it.

"You won't hurt me… Elijah built this down here just in case your grandpa also became like him. He wanted to help him control and take in the wolf as part of him. So tonight we will lock you down here and I will release you in the morning."

So that is why he built this room, I thought to myself. My mom left me and headed back up into the house. I walked over to the cell, running my hands across the bars. The cold steel gave me a chill. I was scared to be locked down here by myself alone. I went back up to find my mom had changed for work. She looked at me, smiled and then left me alone in the house.

I went upstairs to take a quick shower. After I was done, I grabbed my Nike shoes and shorts with a black tank top and decided to go for a run. It has been a while since I ran the woods behind the house like I use to do with my dad. I went outside and did a few stretches before I started to jog into the woods. The smell of the trees around me started to remind me of the races I use to have with dad in these woods. The more and more I thought about it the angrier I became. The anger pushed me I started to run faster and faster. Not realizing how fast I was actually going I made it to the inner pond. When I stopped and looked back I could see the dust in the air starting to settle back on the ground.

I wanted to experiment a little bit so I walked back about a hundred feet looking at the pond in front of me. I took a deep

21

breath and started to run pushing as hard and fast as I could. When I reached the beginning of the pond I launched myself trying to jump the pond. I looked down as I sored across it. I felt like Superman. "I am the king of the..." Before I could finish I found myself falling into the pond just ten feet shy of the shore. I pulled myself out of the pond, dripping wet but my heart was pounding and I loved it. The thrill had me and I soon wanted more.

"Wow, you almost made that jump!" I turned quickly to find a young girl who looked to be younger than me. She was sitting on the giant boulder that overlooked the pond. Her hair was jet black with blonde highlights. I rubbed my eyes because I could not believe how white her skin was, but the thing that stuck out the most was her eyes of blood. I stood frozen just staring at her as she swung her legs back and forth. "What is your name?" She asked me as she giggled.

"Um... Liam," I replied. I started to walk away from her, but before I knew it she was standing in front of me looking up at me.

Her blood-red eyes soon changed to a light violet color. "My name is Mira Tepes, and I think you are cute!" She said to me with a big smile on her face. Something about her was not right. I thought maybe she was like me. But her smell was of something sweet, and she also smelled of death.

"What are you?" I asked her.

She stepped back from me and giggled, "Silly boy I am a vampire!"

When she said that I turned, and I ran as fast as I could. I could hear her running behind me and she was keeping up with no problem. I stopped and then I felt a light tap on my right shoulder.

"Tag your it," she said to me, standing in front of me rocking back and forth on the heels of her feet.

When I looked at her I could see she was older then she acted. She reminded me of my cousin who used to come visit. She used to act the same as this vampire does. "Mira Tepes, right? Hey, how old are you?" I asked her trying to figure her out.

22

"I am five hundred and sixty two years old today actually. It's my birthday!" She said to me.

I was looking at a girl who looked to be fifteen or sixteen years old. How can she be that old? "Well happy birthday. Do you live around here?" I asked her.

"No, I am just out exploring, I live in Seattle, Washington."

My jaw about dropped at the answer she gave me. "You mean to tell me you travelled all the way from Washington State to Alaska just to explore?" I asked her smiling.

"Yep...I needed to get some air. My father was suffocating me."

I could not help it I started to laugh.

"It's not funny, Liam! He would freak if he knew I was talking to a werewolf."

I stood back not even sure how she knew what I was. "How did you know?" I said.

She punched me in the arm. "Silly boy, you smell like wet dog. Only werewolves smell like that after they get wet. I use to know one," she replied.

I heard something in the distance, and when I turned back around Mira was gone, and I was all alone. I headed back to the house. I needed to get back and prepare for tonight. I got home to see my mom's car parked in her spot.

She was home earlier than usual. "Mom you here?" I yelled opening the front door.

"I'm in the den!" She yelled to me.

I walked through the kitchen and into the den. I was surprised to see her in there cleaning up all my dad's baseball stuff. He was born and raised here in Wasilla, Alaska but he loved the San Francisco Giants. I walked in to find the den walls bare; it was

23

once wall-to-wall Giants memorabilia. "Mom what are you doing?" I said stepping into the den.

She turned to look at me as she put the Barry Bonds ball into a box. "Well, it is time that I try and move on a bit. Letting this room stay the way it is will only remind me of your dad and the games we use to go to."

I smiled and then walked over and started helping her put away some of the baseball stuff. After we were done, I looked out to see the night sky and the moon was on the rise. "Liam, I think it's time we get you settled in down stairs."

I looked at my mom and nodded agreeing. I followed behind her to the bookcase and down the stairs to the room below. My mom locked me in the cell and just looked at me crying. "I am so sorry, Liam. I really did not want you to have this life. I prayed and hoped every night for you to be given a normal life."

I grabbed my mom's hands through the cell. "This is not your fault! I do not blame you at all not one bit. I love you, mom," I said to her as I let go of her hand.

She left me heading up the stairs. "I love you, too, Liam!" The metal door closed and I was alone waiting for the wolf to take me over.

"Wow! You live inside a cage?" I turned to see Mira sitting on the ground Indian style. She smiled at me. "How did you get in here? You need to leave. It's not safe!"

Mira got up and then walked over to the cell. "I will not leave you alone down here!" She said, blowing me a kiss. For being over five hundred years old, she was immature.

I looked at Mira and smiled. It made me feel good when she said she would not make me go through this alone. I just looked at her, staring. I couldn't believe how beautiful she was. I dropped to the ground as pain seized my body. I looked up at Mira, tears coming down my face, and my eyes started to hurt. That is when the color changed from hazel to yellow. Mira giggled while looking at me. I started to roll around on the ground as my bones

24

were breaking and resetting. My body started to heat up again. As I started to try and breathe, I heard something. I turned to see Mira humming while watching me. Something strange happened - the humming was actually helping. I could focus in on it helping me set my mind on something else. The pain started to fade - I could feel my bones shifting, but it was not as bad as it started out to be.

In that moment of peace, my humanity disappeared, and I was now just a wolf. I awoke to the feeling of cold cement on my body. I was sore and groggy; my body was aching from the shifting. As I pulled myself up off the ground, I found something taped to the bars. I pulled it off and turned it around it was a photo. Not just any photo. It was of me in my wolf form. It was hard looking at it. I now knew what color wolf I was. I had fur as white as snow. I looked at the bars of the cell, and I could see the dents and teeth marks. I found the towel my mom left me the night before. I wrapped it around my waist in time for my mom to open the door. She was drinking her coffee and smiling.

"How do you feel?"

She asked me. I looked at her. I knew now that I was officially a child of the moon, and that I needed to go.

My mom let me out and I took a shower first. I started to pack my bag as my mom walked in. She looked at me and I could see the tears starting to swell in her eyes

"Are you leaving, Liam?" she asked me.

I looked at her, and I did not want to say the words, it was too hard for me to do. "Mom, I need to leave. I need to learn to control my wolf. When I am able to do this, I promise I will come back," I said to her tossing my leather jacket on. I walked over to her and gave her my jeep keys. "I'm going to take my Ducati, mom, and leave the jeep for you. It was dad's and I think it should stay with you."

I walked down the stairs and out into the garage. Inside was my dad's old '67 Mustang, and next to it was my sixteenth birthday present, a 2008 Ducati. I pulled the cover off of it and tied my pack down on the back. My motorcycle purred to life once I turned it

25

on. Moments later, I was off, leaving everything I knew behind. It was just me and the open road now, but I had an idea where I was going to head.

I was going to find the one who had helped Elijah. I was going to find Hannibal. But first, I wanted to go see Seattle, and find Mira. Just the thought of seeing her again made the long lonely ride worth it. I drove through Canada, and it was just as beautiful as Alaska. I stopped at the Canadian border showing my ID. They let me pass with no problem. The great mountain range called to me; I could feel my new wolf wanting to run and hunt. The call of the wild was powerful, but I wanted to see Mira more than giving in to my wolf.

I stopped in a small town called Forks to put gas in my motorcycle. While there I picked up Mira's scent; it was as clear to me as the road in front of me. I got back on the road and followed her scent until I arrived in the great city of Seattle. It was truly beautiful; the light shined at night like a Christmas tree on Christmas Eve. I followed Mira's scent to a giant mansion just a bit outside of Seattle. It looked like it was old. It might even as old as she was. I turned my bike off, and then pushed the red button on the call box. It beeped twice, and then a female voice answered, "Yes, can I help you?" I leaned in removing my helmet and letting my black hair breathe.

"Um… yes my name is Liam Blackmane, and I am looking for Mira Tepes," I said with politeness in my voice.

The voice went silent for a few moments. "Please come in!" The gate started to open for me. I started my motorcycle back up and slowly made my way to the giant house. I pulled up to an older man wearing a butler's outfit waiting for me. "Welcome to the home of my lord Tepes. Please follow me." I got off my motorcycle and hung my helmet on the clamp on the bike.

I followed behind the butler taking me through a hall that looked to be made of pure gold. Everything in the house looked ancient and very expensive. I felt like this house was a maze. The older gentleman took me to a room that kind of reminded me of my father's office. Except this room was five times as big and had

26

about ten thousand more books. I started to look around the fireplace, which was huge. It was at least ten feet high and five feet wide. I felt so weird there.

"Welcome to my home!" A voice called to me from behind. I turned to find a tall man with pale skin and long white hair. He had on a black suit that looked to be worth as much as my motorcycle. "I am Vlad Tepes, father to Mira Tepes, who you are looking for. Now tell me - why would a child of the moon be looking for my daughter?" he said smiling, showing me his fangs.

"She is my friend, sir," I replied.

He shook his head and poured himself a glass of bourbon I believe.

"FATHER!" I turned to see Mira she was a lovely as ever. She walked passed me and stood in front of her father. "Please do not hurt him... He is a newly born werewolf and I met him while travelling in Alaska," she said to him while turning and smiling at me. Vlad turned his gaze from me to something behind me. I felt something weird, something familiar. I turned and saw a man about my size.

He looked to be around his late twenties but he smelled of my kind. "Hannibal, can you please take this pup with you so that I may have words with my daughter?"

I looked at him and wondered how he came here. "I know you, I read about you!" I said to Hannibal. He looked at me and gestured for me to walk with him. We headed outside the room and through another door into a giant garden. "Tell me, what is this book you speak of is?" he asked me as we walked.

I stopped and looked at him. "My name is Liam Blackmane, and I am the great grandson of Elijah Blackmane." Hannibal went from his fake smile to a straight face. "So you are the descendant of Elijah? What happen to that wolf?" he asked as if he was really interested.

"He was killed in Italy during World War Two," I replied.

27

Hannibal started to laugh, his tone was deep and unwanted. "So I see you are like him, able to become a werewolf without the term of death. How long you been a wolf?"

I looked at him not sure I liked the tone in which he was questioning me. I could hear the arrogance in his voice. "How did you come to be in the service of the vampire lord?" I asked him dodging the questions he asked me.

Hannibal walked over towards the giant fountain in the middle of the garden. "After Elijah disappeared on me and the rest of the pack, we found ourselves under attack by some creatures called Crytosians. They were powerful troll like creatures that killed the entire fort. I was the only one to survive the attack. I went to hunt them down for revenge when I came upon Lord Tepes and his daughter. They had already slayed the Crytosians. I had nothing to live for after that, so Lord Tepes offered me the job of becoming his wolf guard. So I took it, and since then I have been guarding the Tepes family."

Before I could continue my questions Mira was by my side. "Hannibal you are released. My father wants to speak to you," she said with a mischievous smile. Hannibal bowed to Mira and then left us in the garden.

Mira turned and wrapped her arms around me hugging me tight. "I am so glad you are here. I talked to my father and he has agreed to spare your life. But he has one condition!"

I looked at her not sure I liked the sound of that. "And that would be?" I asked her.

She pulled me down close to her so she could whisper into my ear. "He wants you to become my wolf guard, someone who will protect me always."

I was caught off guard. I wanted to say no, but my wolf was going crazy and I could feel how he felt about Mira. "What does it pay?" I asked with a smile. Mira started to laugh and it made me feel good.

Chapter III: Becoming a True Wolfguard

It had been six months since I left home and settled there with Mira. In those last six months I trained with Ronan. He was once the sole wolfguard for the Tepes family. In ancient times werewolves were slaves to the race of the vampiric. Trained to become protectors for the vampires to use as they deemed. After the Great War between the werewolves and vampires, the wolfguard no longer existed. Werewolves and vampires became mortal enemies destined to kill each other. Even though the enslaved werewolves were free, some choose to stay with the vampires.

I walked out of the Dojo after Ronan tossed me around for an hour. I found Mira waiting for me. She looked up at me and smiled. "You okay? I heard you in there screaming like a girl!" She said laughing.

"Oh shut it!" I said smiling.

She got up punched me in the arm like she always did. "I want to go to the mall to shop! Come with me, I need my big bad wolfguard to protect me."

I looked at her taking a deep breath. "Yeah, sure why not… I need to shower first so I will meet you in the main room after I'm done," I replied. I left Mira and headed to my room to shower. I took off my shirt and noticed the bruises that Ronan left. He was a tough teacher, but I was learning. I ran my hand across the bruises, and as I did they started to fade away. I loved being a werewolf; the healing was amazing. As soon as I got into the shower I felt the heat relaxing my tense muscles.

I was starting to enjoy my life there. It was nice and I was still able to enjoy my teenage years. I heard a knock at my bedroom door. I turned off the shower grabbing the towel and wrapping it around my waist. As I opened the door I found Rowan, Mira's older brother. He looked at me with his deep blue eyes. His blonde hair was always kept up in a ponytail. Even though he was next in line for the Tepes throne, he always treated me with respect. "Hey, what's up Rowan?" I said opening the door to let him enter.

29

Rowan passed by me patting my bare shoulder; the cold of his touch giving me the chills. He walked over and then sat on the sofa, tossing his legs up on the table.

"I am just stopping by to say bye. I am heading back to London to take over the family's controlling interests in a tech firm there. I just wanted to thank you again for looking out for my baby sister. Even though she is over five hundred years old, she still needs someone to look out for her. If you were not here, I would have to take her with me and for that I owe you one."

I walked into my walk-in closet and grabbed some clothes to toss on. "Do not even worry about it, Rowan. I hope you enjoy it there. Maybe I will have come visit you sometime after Ronan think's I am wolf enough to be on my own," I said pulling my black tee shirt over my head. I tossed on some boxers and my faded blue jeans walking out of the closet. Rowan got up and walked over to me, handing me a key.

"I want you to have my 1967 Impala. I won't be taking it with me, and I do not plan on coming back for a long time." I looked down at the key. I knew how much he loved that car. He had it since it was new. We bumped knuckles and he left me in the room. I tossed on my black Nike shoes and then headed down to the main room. Mira was sitting on the couch holding her head in her hands like a little girl. I knew she was all woman, but it was hard to look at her in that way. "Let's go!" I said standing in front of her. She looked up at me rising to her feet.

"You are so yummy!" She said licking her red lips. I took her by her hand and we headed out. I decided to take the Impala, since it was parked outside. It's black paint was untouched. Rowan kept the car in perfect shape.

Mira stopped in front of the car. "Um, we can't take Rowans car, he will kill us!" She said looking at me.

I laughed and pulled the key from my pocket, "He gave it to me today."

Mira started to jump up and down. "Hell, yeah, lets hit the road!"

30

I was caught off guard by how she was acting. I unlocked the doors and started the car; it roared to life and I loved it.

Mira looked at me with the biggest smile on her face. "I have never been in the Impala, so be gentle. It's my first time," she said buckling her safety belt.

I put the car in gear and let the tires burn out. The ride was sweet and I loved it. I took the long way to get into Seattle. I did not want to end the ride, it was nice - just me and Mira being out together. I enjoyed having her next to me. I pulled up parking outside of the mall entrance. I got out and let Mira out.

"What a gentleman," she said stepping out of the car.

"Anything for you, ma'am!" I replied closing her door. We walked into the mall hand in hand. Our first stop was Build-a-Bear. She wanted a new stuff animal. She picked out the grey wolf and named it Liam. After that it felt as if we went to every store. When the day was at an end, I had a dozen bags I was carrying for her. We went back to the car. The back seat was covered in all her bags. "Thank you, Liam, for coming with me today! I think tomorrow we should start the bond between us."

I started the car and headed back to the manor. "What do you mean bond?" I asked her.

Mira looked out the window running her fingers across it. "It is what will link us for life. Through the bond you can call upon my energy to shift anytime you want. The full moon will no longer hold her control over you. Also, when I am in trouble you will know and be able to locate me."

I let my eyes leave the road for a moment just so I could look at her. She turned and looked back at me with her beautiful eyes. "I will do anything to be with you forever!" I said with a smile, returning my attention back to the road. I watched Mira reach for the radio. As she turned it on I was surprised to hear the music that was on. It was the Zac Brown Band. I had no idea Rowan was a country fan. We pulled up to the house and the butler was standing there waiting for us. He opened Mira's door and then started to collect her bags. I was glad he was there. I did not want to have to

31

unpack them, too. I started to follow Mira into the house when I heard Ronan. "Liam, I need you to come with me," he said running his hands across his bald head.

Every time I saw Ronan, I thought I was in church. He was once a priest, but he does not follow the faith any longer. But he does wear a priest uniform minus the white color part.

"Where we going?" I asked him, turning to follow him instead of going into the house.

"Just shut your yap and follow me. No more questions!"

I closed my mouth making a zipping sound with my hand. We walked past the Dojo and into the woods that surrounded the house. It was dark so I called upon my wolf and shifted my eyes. I could now see in the dark. I soon found a giant temple in front of us. It looked old, even older then the Tepes manor. Ronan looked around and then pushed a brick in on the side of the temple. A door appeared on the side of the temple, and I followed him slowly, not sure where he was taking me. The passage led to a room that was as big as the main room in the mansion. Inside were five giant statues of werewolves. Ronan walked over to the one in the middle.

"These five wolves were the five children of the great spirit of the moon. They are our forefathers and we are their children. I brought you here because I know about the blood pact that Mira wants you to perform. I know when you look at Mira you see a beautiful young lady, but the truth is she is a killer. Many years ago, she was called the Princess of Blood. She would wipe whole villages out in one night. Mira was the black thorn born of the Tepes bloodline, even the lord Tepes feared for her. He knew that her blood thirst was something that could not be controlled. Yes, through the blood pact you will no longer answer to the moon, but in that you will never be free from her. You will replace one chain for another. I was once tied to the wife of the Lord Tepes. I was her personal protector, her wolfguard. For over a thousand years I lived for her, and only her. On the night of her death, I was scarred for life."

32

I watched Ronan drop his black coat on the ground. On his back was a set of long scars that looked to be claw marks.

"See these scars? They are called the Abu-ra, a curse placed upon us once we fail to protect our charges. These marks block my connection with my wolf, and I can no longer call upon him. I have lost him forever!"

I was stunned at everything Ronan was saying, but his sadness spread over me like a blanket. I started to think about what the price was. Did I really want that to lose my wolf forever? Ronan walked over and reached up touching the paw of the middle wolf.

"Did you know that one?"

Ronan turned around and looked at me. "This is my forefather, he is the beginning of my bloodline."

I started to wonder which one of those wolves was my family. I walked over starring up at all the wolves. They looked so graceful and powerful. "How did you know that wolf was your forefather?" I asked.

Ronan turned around and walked over to the small fountain in the back of the room. "These are the tears of the Great Spirit. When I found this temple I was mad with grief and sadness. I took part in the tasting of the water. It gave me a vision and showed me every wolf in my bloodline! That also is including Roma, my forefather."

I walked over to stand next to Ronan, looking down at these magical waters. I looked over at him.

"Do you want to see where you come from?" Ronan asked me.

The thought of it was tempting to me, but I was not ready for that kind of insight! I backed away turning to leave the hidden room.

"Liam… Do not tell the Lord of this place, he will surely destroy it. In here lies the truth to us, and all the knowledge of the ancients."

33

I looked back at Ronan, gazing at him. I turned and then left the room stepping outside and taking in a deep breath of air. The half-moon hung in the starry sky like a hook on a fishing pole. I decided to take a walk, letting the thoughts of tonight fade away. The choice of becoming a wolfguard was a heavy burden I was not sure I was ready to have. I was only eighteen years old and I still had not lived. Did I really want to be bonded to Mira for all of my immortal life? I was not sure how much time had passed, but the moon was now set in a different position in the night's sky. I stopped, finding myself standing on a cliff that over looked the great Pacific Ocean. I raised my hands to the sky wishing in that moment I could fly. I was lost in the thought of it and I did not hear her come up on me. I turned to see a wolf, but not just any wolf. This one glowed like the moon.

"I heard your cries for help," I heard the voice of a female, but I was not sure where it was coming from. The wolf soon started to radiate with a blinding light. I had to turn my gaze from her. When the light dimmed I no longer found a glowing wolf, but now a female with white robes and a slight glow to her.

"I am she from whom all werewolves are born. I have come because your pain was so great it called to me. As I look upon you, I can see my son Tier in you. He was my eldest son and the most powerful of my five children. Tier was a great warrior. He spent his immortal life watching over the tribe he had created. I know of the offer the dead one gave you, and I feel the sorrow you have for the one you call Ronan. I cannot tell you that I forbid you from doing what she asked you. But I can tell you that to break one bond and build another, you will lose something."

"When my children started to be used by the vampires, I went to the god of them and told her. My children were not created to be her children's personal play things. So the vampire god and I came to the terms that she would use her power to help release my children. But she created the blood pact, which is a way for her children to still use my children. When I found out about it, I created the Abu-ra, a curse that will take the wolf from them leaving them marked forever without the true gifts of the wolf."

34

I looked at her. I was still lost in her power; I could feel it and it felt like the energy I received from the moon. She walked over, catching my eyes with her gaze. I felt the warmth of her hands touch my face.

"My son loved you all. Remember being blessed with the wolf is a most sacred and honorable right. Do not give up that for a bond with a being that is not alive nor is dead." She leaned in and kissed my forehead. When I opened my eyes I was alone on that cliff once again. I turned and headed back to the house. I passed by the night watch without them even seeing me.

I climbed into bed and just let the silence of the night take me away. I soon was sleeping as sound as I did when I was a baby. As morning came I heard a soft knock at my bedroom door. By the scent in the air I knew it was Mira. I pulled the covers off of me. I noticed I was still wearing the clothes from the night before. As I opened the door Mira looked at me with a smile, but for some reason I was not able to return the favor.

"What's wrong with you Liam?"

I looked at her, everything I learned last night still weighed heavily on my mind. "I am okay, just a rough night. What's up?"

Mira's smile disappeared and she just looked at me with a blank face. I was not sure but I could have sworn I picked up the scent of anger on Mira. I felt a force on the door and Mira passed under me entering my room. She jumped on my bed rolling around on it looking at me. "I am going to get in the shower, Mira," I said to her. She just smiled at me and watched me enter the bathroom.

I turned the shower on letting the steam fill the bathroom while I peeled the clothes off from last night. As soon as the water hit my body I felt a bit of peace and calm flow over me. My wolf was slumbering and I almost felt like I did before I became a werewolf. The heat from the water felt relaxing like always. I stepped out of the shower grabbing my new towel the butler set up for me. I walked out forgetting Mira was on my bed. There I stood naked with Mira's eyes growing as she looked at me. I quickly wrapped my towel around my waist trying not to blush.

35

Mira started to giggle getting up off the bed. "When you are more dressed, meet me in the theatre room. It's movie day and I want to watch one of my favorites with you." Mira raised her hand blowing me a kiss before leaving my room.

I got dressed putting on a new white tee shirt and some boxers. I put on the same pants from the night before along with some socks and my black hiking boots.

I headed downstairs running into Hannibal. He was coming from one of the maid's chambers. "Hannibal, do you have a minute?"

He looked at me and smiled. "What's up, Blackmane?" He said buttoning his black shirt.

From what I could tell he was doing a bit of off the books fun.

"What do you know about the Abu-ra?"

His smile left his face. Soon it was a face that lacked emotion. "Where did you hear about that?" he said with rage in his voice.

"It doesn't matter… you know what, forget it." I turned and headed back down the stairs. I could feel Hannibal's eyes still on me. I walked to the first floor entering into the theatre room. Mira was sitting waiting for me. She had a cup that smelled of blood and some popcorn. I took the seat next to her. "So what are we watching today?" I asked.

She looked at me smiling like always. "No talking in the theatre. Sit back and enjoy the movie."

I turned my head to the screen; the music starting to play and I knew exactly what I was. I laughed and she looked at me.

"And what is so funny, mister?" she asked.

"Really, we are going to watch 'The Godfather'?" I said with a smile on my face. I was not expecting her to like this kind of movie.

"Hell, yes! 'The Godfather' kicks ass!" She said turning her attention back to the screen.

I sat watching the movie, but it was hard for me. I remembered the last time I saw it. I was with my dad back at home hanging out in the den. That day we had a giant popcorn fight; it was a good day. I got up leaving Mira in the theatre room. I needed to get some air. I walked out of the house to find Lord Tepes grooming his roses in the front.

"Hello Liam. I can sense that your heart is in a state of loss. What troubles you?"

I walked over to stand next to him. He was the most powerful vampire alive, but he was so gentle with the flowers.

"I just have so much to think about. Things I never thought I would have to deal with at my age. I always thought I would live my life going to college and becoming a doctor like my dad was." He cut a rose from the bush handing it to me. "What is this for?" I asked.

He arose up from his knees brushing off his tan pants. For being the Lord of Darkness he sure did wear some light colored clothes. He had tan pants, tan sandals and a white pull over shirt. "Sometimes you need to just stop and smell the roses. But tonight is the eclipse and you need to save your energy for the blood pact." I knew in that moment he did not really care anything about me. I was just a pawn for him to move around as he saw fit. I got up and started to walk into the giant garden that took up half the estate. I enjoyed the garden the most of this place because it was relaxing and very beautiful.

"Why did you leave?" I turned to find Mira sitting on the brick wall next to the stargazers.

"Sorry, just memories of my dad. Hey, can we talk about tonight?" I asked her.

"Sure, you can always talk to me about everything. What's on your mind?" She looked so innocent to me, but what Ronan said

37

about her stuck with me. I forgot that vampires are savage beings. And she was no different. She was one of them.

"I am not sure I am ready to take on the eternal task of being a wolfguard. I have found out some new things about becoming a wolfguard. I learned that if you were to die after we were bound I would lose my wolf. I would never be able to shift again."

Mira looked at me I could see sadness in her eyes. But I could also feel anger coming from her. "I can understand your fears but I am no mere vampire. I am the daughter of the first vampire. I am Mira Tepes, eternal queen of all vampires." She just looked at me, her eyes as red as blood again. The rage flowed over her and I could feel her power. It was like nothing I had ever felt before. I could feel my wolf, he was riled up. He wanted blood and he wanted Mira's blood. She could tell too because she looked at me with fear in her eyes.

"Mira… I care for you so much it hurts to think about you not in my life. But the fear of losing who I am scares me more."

Mira jumped off the wall and stood there looking at me. Her red eyes faded back to the violet they usually were. "I will be here tonight at the time of the eclipse. If you come I will know you love me and if you don't, I will understand." She turned and walked away from me. I think what she said was the most grown up thing she had said since I have known her. After she left I turned, exiting the garden and starting to walk deep in the forest. I kept walking past the temple. I still wondered how that temple was never seen by the humans. The forest was so beautiful, and it put my wolf at peace when I spent time in it. This was my home. No, this is our home.

The air was cool and the smell of the woods added to my enjoyment. Even before I became a werewolf I loved the woods. I loved fishing and hunting with my father. I missed him. I looked up into the webs that the branches of the trees weaved. Taking in a deep breath, the once crisp sweet air was tainted. The air had the smell of blood in it. I followed it to find to my sadness. It was Ronan. He was dead lying on the cliff. His limp hand hung over it.

38

He was faced down in a puddle of mud and blood. I ran to him, rolling Ronan on to his back. I stepped back to see his body was mutilated, his guts hanging from his stomach out onto the ground. I could smell the scent of vampire all over him. But this scent was not familiar to me. I had never smelt this one before.

I left Ronan there, running back to the Manor. I pushed through the front doors and made my way to the parlor room. I found Lord Tepes and three other new vampires sitting sipping on their cups of blood. I soon picked up the same scent that was on Ronan's dead body. I looked around until I saw him, the one who killed Ronan. He was about 6 feet tall, with broad shoulders. He was built like a truck. He kind of reminded me a bit of Mark. This vampire had a long scar running down his right eye. Something he got before becoming a vampire. His hair had the color of light blue mixed with his white hair.

The rage took over me and I gave into my wolf. I took off charging at the vampire grabbing him and slamming him into the wall behind him. He looked at me hissing. I could feel my blood, it was boiling and I wanted him dead. I started to growl at him and I could feel my face shifting before I could do anymore to him. I felt a strong hand grab me and toss me across the room. I smashed into the wall falling onto a chair. I jumped up letting out a loud growl that echoed through the house. I stood face to face with Lord Tepes and I knew it was a futile fight, but I could not let that vampire live.

"YOU WILL CALM YOURSELF, DOG! OR I WILL KILL YOU HERE AND NOW!"

I felt the power in his voice. It did not affect me in the slightest, but I knew he was right. I was no match for him.

I soon felt a hand on my arm. I turned and Mira stood next to me. She looked at me with concern in her eyes. "Please, Liam, calm down… I do not want to lose you!" In her voice I could feel the sadness she felt when she said that to me. I took a deep breath backing away letting my body rest. My face soon returned to normal, my eyes were now there usual hazel color. I looked over at the vampire I attacked. He smiled straightening out his shirt. His red eyes still had the color of blood in them. He had fed on Ronan before he killed him.

"Why did you kill Ronan?" I yelled to the vampire.

He looked at me and then turned his attention to Lord Tepes. "Ronan has been due for his punishment for failing the royal family. On his watch he let the queen be killed. It was in my right to take the punishment into my own hands. Do not worry, he fought back. Then again, he was only half a wolf now, wasn't he!" he said laughing.

I glared at him. I was beginning to become enraged again. Mira grabbed onto me snuggling into my arm. I turned and just walked away pulling away from Mira. I left. I needed to go back and bury Ronan. I arrived to find him where I left him. I spent an hour digging his grave. I rolled him up in a black blanket and buried him in the ground. I made a marker out of stones next to the temple. I thought he would be happy being buried next to it. I looked up to see that the eclipse was happening. In that moment I knew I had to pick. Either become Mira's wolfguard or don't, it was a hard choice.

I knew in my heart that Mira loved me, but did I really love her, too? I ran back. I had made my choice - I wanted to be with Mira. I arrived in the garden to find her smiling, sitting on a rock.

"I knew you would never leave me," she said, jumping up and hugging me.

"So how do we do this thing?" I asked her.

She let go of me and looked at me with her violet eyes. "Do you accept me?" she asked. Our gazes had locked, and I could not take my eyes from hers.

"I do!" I replied.

Mira took my hand, biting down on it. I could feel her fangs sinking in, and a cool sensation spread through my body. I was lost in the intoxication of the bite; there was nothing like it. Mira released my hand from her fangs. She looked at me, using her nail

40

to make a small cut on her wrist. "Drink," she said offering me her wrist. I closed my eyes, taking her wrist into my mouth and letting her blood flow down my throat.

In that moment, the eclipse passed, and I felt a new type of energy flowing through me. I felt even more alive than I did on the night I became one with my own wolf. In that moment, I became her guardian, her true wolfguard.

Chapter IV: Ancient Promises

It has been a year since the blood pact between Mira and I was completed. We left Washington State behind and returned to Alaska. I came back to see my mom, but it was too late for that. I found out that my mom passed away over a year ago. She died of a broken heart, which was my fault because I left her behind. All I had of my mother was the house and her gravesite in Wasilla.

I went to visit my mom's gravesite, and Mira was not happy about it. "If you go, I cannot come with you!" I looked at her, not sure what she was talking about.

"What do you mean you cannot come with me?" I asked her.

She twisted her hair with her fingers. "Cemeteries are placed on holy ground. Being a vampire, I am forbidden from stepping on holy ground. If I do, it will cause me great pain, and in the end, I will be killed."

I looked at her and smiled. "Well, it sucks to be you!" I said, laughing.

Mira crossed her arms and just stared at me. "Sometimes I really hate you!" she said trying not to smile.

"I will be back in an hour," I said walking past her.

She grabbed my arm and looked up at me. "Please hurry back I hate when you are not around."

I smiled at her as I walked out the door. I took my motorcycle and headed out. The drive was not too long. It took me about two hours to reach Wasilla from Anchorage. My mom was buried at the Crescent Moon Cemetery. I found her grave at the top of the hill next to my dad's. It was hard seeing them both dead. I hated myself for not being here for her. "Mom, I am so sorry I was not here for you. If I would have known me leaving would have done this to you, I would have never left you. I love you and Dad so much." I started to feel weird, as if someone was watching me. I looked around but found no one.

42

"It's not your fault this happened."

I jumped up looking around. "Who said that?" I said taking a sniff of the air. I would know if someone were there, I would pick up their scent. But to my amazement there was nothing. I started to think I was going crazy. I turned to look back at my parent's grave and kneeling next to them was a stranger in a black cloak. "Who are you?" I said reaching for the stranger. But something happened I did not expect. My hand went through the stranger. I backed away a bit, not sure what this stranger was. The hooded stranger turned removing the hood.

Standing before me was a young blacked headed beauty. She looked at me and smiled. "Please do not be afraid. I am Celeste, and I am your sister." I looked at her wide-eyed.

I was becoming angry. I hated people messing with my family or me. "I would advise you to not start ridiculous lies. I would have known if I had a sister!" I said with a low growl.

She dropped the cloak, and as it hit the ground it turned to black smoke. She looked at me with her white eyes. She had no color to them. They looked like that of a person suffering from blindness. "I was born before you and I died before you were born. On my thirteenth birthday I was mauled and killed by a bloodthirsty vampire. She was a monster. Her violet eyes turned to red before she took me for her next meal."

Once I became a werewolf, I gained certain abilities and one of them was detecting the truth or a lie. As I looked at her I could only detect what she was saying to be the truth. If it was true what she said, then the vampire who took her life was Mira. But why would she not tell me this? "How come it took you this long to show yourself to me?" I asked the ghost.

Celeste looked at me and pointed to my mother's grave. "When I died I watched as mother and father buried me. I did not move on, I could not. As time passed I started to notice I could do things. It was on the day they brought you home that I first appeared. I stood there like I am now with you and mother looking at me. She reached for me, walking through me. I looked down at you in your

43

crib and I knew right away, you would one day become a wolf. The aura around you was strong and outlined you with that of the wolf. I think mother thought I was going to hurt you. So she called Sage and I soon found myself blocked from the house and you. As time passed I was contacted by the angel of death himself. He offered me the job of reaper and I took it. I stand here because I was the reaper who took mom."

Celeste turned and looked down at the graves. I could have sworn I heard her start to cry, but can ghosts really cry? I walked over and stood next to her. I felt a cold chill run through me. I looked down and I could see her hand trying to take mine. "So what happens next?" I asked.

Celeste moved away from me pulling out a pendant that she wore. It looked like a black heart, like a real human heart. She tore the necklace from her neck. She dropped it on the ground and it vanished. "I am now free, no longer bound to do my duties as a reaper. I think I will come with you back to your home."

I was not sure that would be good since I lived and loved the vampire who killed her. "How does that work?"

Celeste walked over to me. She spotted the wolfguard pendant I wore. Celeste reached up and touched my pendant making it glow. Then, before my eyes, she disappeared. I started to look around but I could not find her. "Celeste?" I yelled but she did not answer.

I went back to my bike and headed back home. I really did miss Mira but I was also upset at her. She killed my sister. It took me a little less than two hours to get home. I pulled up to find a black Bentley parked outside. I pulled my helmet off, took a deep breath and, sure enough, there were new vampires. I walked into the house and sitting in the living room was Mira and three other vampires.

Two of the vampires stood around like guards. As for the other, he sat across from Mira and had on a very expensive black suit. His hair was short blonde and kept neat. Mira looked up at me with sadness in her eyes. Then the gaze of the vampire left Mira and settled in on me. "Aw, look! Your pet dog has finally come home.

44

He must not be a great wolfguard if he leaves you alone for so long."

"Who are you and what are you doing here?" I commanded with power and rage in my voice. The two guards started to move, but the vampire sitting down raised his hand. The other two stopped at his command.

"Oh, how terribly rude of me. I am Duncan Craven, and I am Mira's husband!" I soon passed anger and went into rage.

I looked down at Mira. She would not return the gaze. I started to let my wolf free, and I could feel the change start to happen. I was going to kill everything in this room, but something inside me stopped me. A voice, a female voice. "Liam, do not give into the vampire. He wants you to. He wants you to attack so he can kill you!" I soon realized it was Celeste talking to me. "Mira, is it true? Is what this vampire says true?" I asked looking at her.

She looked up at me her violet eyes had tears in them. "Yes… We were married over four hundred years ago. It was my father's will that we became wife and husband. But after the wedding, Duncan left. I had not seen him since." I looked up at this Duncan Craven, my eyes as yellow as the sun and burning for his blood.

"Mira, it is time that you and I come together. It is time you give me a child, an heir to my families' fortune and your royal family." Duncan rose up, walking towards Mira.

I could not help it. I stepped between her and him. He looked at me, his eyes as red as blood. I could feel his anger, but my wolf was enjoying it, so was I.

"How dare you come between my wife and me. If you value your life I suggest you move!"

I just looked at him. I was not going to move. "I am sworn to protect my lady and if that means from you to then so be it. I suggest you leave now before I really get mad!"

Duncan looked at me and then smiled. "Trained this one well, didn't you, Mira? Hope you keep this one alive longer than your

45

last dog!" he said walking around me and out the door. I turned and the other two followed him.

I turned and looked at Mira. "We need to talk and now!" I said walking into the kitchen pouring some orange juice. I sat down on the bar seat next to the counter. Mira got up and walked over just looking at me. "I have learned so many disturbing things about you today. First, I found out you killed my sister. Second, I find out I am not your first wolfguard!"

Her face changed from sadness to utter disbelief. I do not think she expected me to know anything about my sister. Mira looked at me with a blank expression on her pale face. "You need to understand something, Liam. I am very old so in my time, yes, I have had another wolfguard. His name was Gideon and he was with me for over two hundred years. The only reason he is not with me now is because of my father. He had him killed because Gideon was not as loyal as he said he was. He tried to end my life while I slept. As for your sister, I was taken over by the thirst. I could not fight it. I tried my best but in the end it won out and, yes, I took her life!"

I got up from the stool looking down I saw my necklace. It was glowing bright red and then she appeared, my dead sister. Celeste looked at me and smiled, then turned and stared at Mira. "I felt your pain and I can see the sorrow in your heart. I wanted to tell you that I do forgive you for what you did."

Mira looked at me and I could see worry in her eyes. "How come you did not tell me that your sister has possessed you?"

I was not even sure what she meant. How did my sister possess me, she lived in my necklace not in me. "What are you talking about?" I asked Mira.

She walked over to me just passing through Celeste, as if she was not there. "Liam, your sister has linked to you. This means she will stay with you until she decides to leave. She will feed on you, your energy and in that she can feed on me, too."

I looked passed Mira and at my sister. I could not imagine my sister hurting me in anyway. She was my sister and family is

46

everything to me. "Mira, you are wrong, she would never feed on me." As Mira turned to look at Celeste, I could feel the rage coming from Mira. Celeste just stood there smiling at Mira, not letting it bother her.

"I think that I need some time away on my own! I need to rethink my life and us." Mira looked at me with the sadness falling onto her face. I could tell I just said something she never wanted to hear.

She backed up from me slowly tears coming from her eyes. "I will not force you to stay. If you need some time, I will honor that," she said to me with a trembling voice.

I walked over to Mira kissing her on the forehead. Celeste started to glow and then she flowed back into my necklace. I grabbed my coat and then walked out the door. I got on my bike and took off hitting the road. I did not look back once.

Days passed and I just kept driving; only stopping for food and fuel. I soon found myself across the United States stopping in Maine. Some town called Wolf Creek, it was beautiful town covered by the green forest and next to the coast. I stopped at a small diner that overlooked the marina of the town. It was peaceful and it was what I was looking for. After having lunch I looked around town. The air was crisp and cool. It had the taste of the sea and forest in it. I found a small cottage on the edge of town that I rented. As the sun set, I decided to check out all of the town and its surroundings. I shifted and started to explore the forest.

I spent time hunting a deer, it was fun and I enjoyed it immensely as did my wolf. After I was done, I spent the rest of my time exploring taking in my new territory when I came upon something I never expected to find, a light brown female werewolf. Her scent was the same as the roses that surrounded my cottage. She looked at me with her yellow gaze, just as lost as mine. I walked slowly towards her. She stepped back baring her teeth a bit. I could feel the fear she had towards me.

I dropped my head taking my eyes off her. I was trying to show her she had nothing to fear. I soon felt her cold nose press against

47

my head. She was taking in my scent. I raised my head slowly. Our noses touched, then she backed up an inch still looking at me. I howled and saw her ears lower. She felt my power. I was a born alpha and she was not. I stood back a bit shifting in front of her, trying to help her understand I won't hurt her.

I stood there naked feeling the cold breeze run up my backside. She started to circle around me. I felt like bait and she was the shark. I hated feeling like this and so did my wolf but I knew I had to do this. It was the only way she would feel safe around me. I looked at her. The moonlight shined down on her making her even more stunning. She turned and took off running away from me. I stood there watching her leave. I knew I would find her again. I started to head back to the cottage - alone and naked. I reached the cottage and called it a night.

As I fell asleep, the only thing on my mind was the female werewolf. I awoke to a light tapping coming from my front door. I got up still naked. I approached the door and I immediately picked up a scent that smelled of rage and anger. I grabbed my pants from the chair next to the door, putting them on before opening it.

Standing before me was a tall muscular man with short blonde hair and a beard. His eyes had the color of turquois in them. His skin was rough looking, almost like leather. "Can I help you?" I asked him. He pushed passed me entering into the cottage. "Sure, come on in!" I turned and he was sniffing the air when it hit me. The scent was werewolf, he was like me.

"I am Bayne, alpha of the Wolf Creek pack. I was told about you by my sister, Nyssa. She said she ran into you last night. What brings you to my territory?"

I walked passed him, this time pouring myself some orange juice. I turned and he was standing right behind me. "I came here to clear my head... I have no intent of causing you any problems!"

Bayne turned around and walked over to the mantle above the fireplace. He picked up a photo that came with the cottage. "It has been seventy years since I last stood in this place. My grandma use to live here when I was a young boy. I want you to come to the bar

48

tonight, it's down on Main Street next to the docks." Bayne turned around leaving and taking the photo with him.

I started to breathe slowly trying to keep my wolf calm. I cooked some breakfast and decided to grab a fishing pole and head down to the beach. The sand felt good on my bare feet. It has been years since I had been to a beach. The waves came in crashing. I found three or four other people. They were all fishing. I found a quite spot away from them. I needed space. "Liam, be careful tonight please. That wolf was a baddy." I grabbed on to my necklace, it kind of freaked me out a bit. I almost forgot she was there. I had not heard her voice since leaving Alaska.

I spent the whole day down at the beach. It was boring and not something I would usually do, but it was peaceful. I did not catch anything, so I packed up and headed back to the cottage. I took a quick shower and got dressed. It was about time to head to the bar. I put on my blue jeans, black button down shirt and boots. I got on my bike and then headed down to the bar. It was called the Wolves Den. There were Harleys parked outside it, many of them. I parked my Ducati next to a blue and red Harley. "Nice bicycle kid!" I turned to see a fat biker looking at me. He smiled at me than started to laugh. I took off my helmet locked it to my bike. By the smell of the fat biker as I passed him entering into the bar, he was human.

I started to look around. It was packed and looked like a rundown bar. I was surprised to see a place like this in a peaceful town, but here it was. I went to the bar and a black-headed bartender with tattoos all over her body looked at me. "What do you want, little boy?" she asked.

What is it with everyone giving me crap? "Give me a corona with lime!"

She nodded and then pulled out the beer placing a lime on the mouth of the bottle. "Glad to see you have your clothes on!"

I turned with my beer in my hand. I found a beautiful woman with a slender build. She wore a black halter-top and faded blue jeans with black boots. Her hair was light brown and eyes the color

49

of the ocean. The most beautiful part of her was her skin tone. It had a honey color to it. "Why, hello!" I said.

She looked at me grabbing my beer. I watched her chug it down like a champ. "Thanks for the beer... I think you should come with me, the real party is in the back!" I followed her through the crowed. She opened a door and we went in. I soon found myself in a back room with seven other people. By the scents of them they were the pack of the town. Bayne sat up from the table in the back walking over to me. "Glad you can make it, Liam!" he said slapping my shoulder. "You made it just in time. We were just about to head out and take a midnight run." Bayne and the rest started to head out the back door.

Nyssa looked at me holding her hand out for me to take. This was all new for me. I was not used to being around my own kind. "Come on, I won't bite... much that is!" I grabbed her hand and she pulled me along like I was a puppy.

I walked out with Nyssa to see the pack undressing in the alleyway behind the bar. Bayne looked over at me as he removed his shirt showing his six-pack. I shook my head and found Nyssa next to me almost naked. This was a sight I could not take my eyes from. She smiled at me pointing her finger to the night sky. I looked up noticing the moon was full again for the second night in a row. I heard the pack making the noises of shifting. Nyssa was on all fours. I could see her bones breaking and moving under her skin. Baynes' yellow gaze was set on me, and I could see his look of confusion and loss in them. I was no longer bound to the power of the moon.

I was soon surrounded by seven wolves, all looking at me. I looked around and found the grey and white wolf pushing through the pack. It was Bayne. He was showing his dominance over the pack. I turned around and Nyssa was whimpering at me. I gave in to her. I stripped and started to shift. Since bonding with Mira I shifted almost instantly, no delay or pain. I stretched out smiling at Nyssa as she butted heads with me. Bayne pushed passed me, hitting me with his broad shoulders. I shook it off and took off behind him. We hit the beach running. The cold of the sand felt even better on my paws than on my human feet.

The sensation of running with a pack was something I had never felt before. I could feel the energy that came from the pack, it was amazing. I spent the whole night running with them. I loved having Nyssa next to me. She never left me, not once.

During the night the pack ran like one unit, it was almost like a military unit. As the night started to fade away the sunlight started to shine down on the pack. The shift started and I was already done while they still went through it. The pack finished the shift and they lay there on the cold, damp, wet moss and grass of the woods. Bayne looked at me noticing I was already standing, which made him try and get up. I could tell me standing was a powerful sign to him, it made him feel weak.

Bayne came to his feet a bit wobbly but becoming steady. "What is your deal? How can you shift instantly and not feel the pain like the rest of us?" he asked with a heavy breath.

I wanted to tell him but wolfguard law forbids it. "I have always been able to do this!" I replied with a lie.

Bayne shook his head pushing passed me. The rest of the pack got up slowly and started to follow him. Nyssa did not at first, but Bayne turned and looked at her. She dropped her head and got in line like a good doggy.

I started to follow them back to the bar. I got dressed and headed back to the cottage, it was still early. I arrived back at the cottage to find a black SUV parked outside. I picked up the scents of five vampires and one werewolf. I opened the door to find Lord Tepes and Hannibal sitting on the couch. The other four vampires gathered behind their master. He did not look too happy seeing me. I walked over and stood in front of Lord Tepes and Hannibal. "What brings you to my humble abode?" I asked with a smile.

"You failed my daughter as her wolfguard. Because of you she was taken by the council of elders. She is being punished for my actions. I want her back and you are going to do that!"

The power in his voice ran chills up my back. I could feel it like touching my own skin and he was pissed. I knew I had no choice in the matter. "Where should I start looking?" I said.

Hannibal rose up from the couch. "Go to San Francisco. You will find a weretiger there. His name is Zander. He can point you in the direction of the council." I nodded and turned, going to the room. I got dressed in the clothes from the night before and got on the Ducati. I left heading back into a life I was not ready to go back to. I knew I had to find her. I might be mad at her, but I loved her, I truly did.

As I left Wolf Creek behind, I grew sad. I was also forced to leave Nyssa. There was something about her that made everything else not matter. I started to push harder, trying to get to California quicker. Then I heard something. It sounded like Mira echoing through my head. I forgot we had the telepathic bond. Hearing her voice made me angry, knowing I left her and now she is in danger. I swore to protect her and failed at my job as her wolfguard.

Chapter V: Sins Of The Father

As I arrived in town I picked up a scent of a vampire. That led me back to a club called Kitty's Pride. It was snuggled in the back of an alley way and it smelled horribly of cats. I parked my motorcycle on the street. It was weird, I felt like I had eyes on me.

I walked down the alley and was stopped. Standing before me was a body builder. He was huge and had on a shirt that looked to be four times too small for him. His hair was the color of an orange and he had on tiny shorts. I stood there trying to keep my laughter contained.

"No dogs allowed!" he said with a deep voice.

I turned looking around, "Dogs? I do not see any dogs here!"

The sweating to the oldies reject used his index finger to poke me in the chest. "You are the dog, werewolf!" he said with a wide smile.

"Okay, you got me. I am a werewolf, oh no… How about you just step aside and we can stay friends," I said, trying to pass him. He stuck his huge trunk of an arm out blocking me. I stepped back looking at him. "Okay… now you are trying my patience! If you want to keep that arm I would advise you to keep it to yourself." He looked at me his eyes changed from brown to that of a cat. He started to laugh; his whole body shook as he did. "By your smell you are new, so I think you might want to hold your tone. I have killed many of your kind in my six hundred years of living. What do you want with my Khan, Zander?" His Khan… is that what his leader is called?

"I was sent here by the Lord of Vampires to talk to your Khan!" He stepped back away from me turning to let me pass. I walked past him and he dropped his head, not looking at me. I walked down opening the club door and going in. Looking around, it looked like your run of a mill strip club. However, by the scents in the room, there was more weretigers than humans in it. I looked around until I spotted him. He turned, looking at me from the bar. He had the looks of someone in his twenties. His physique was that of a swimmer, and his skin tone was that of Native American

53

decent. His hair was blonde and hung down to the middle of his back.

He walked over, making his way through the crowd. But it was not him who had to move, the crowd moved out of his way. He soon stood in front of me wearing black slacks, loafers and a white button down shirt. "How did you get into my club, wolf?" he asked with his perfect smile.

I looked at him not even sure how he could be so perfect. "I was sent here by Vlad Tepes, lord of the vampires. He said you could point me in the direction of the council. I need to find them to save Mira Tepes, his daughter. She is also my charge, I am her wolfguard."

He looked at me with green eyes. "Well, you must be Liam, then… Hannibal told me all about you. The wolfguard who is in love with his charge. I need you to do something for me first. I do not give out info for free!"

I looked at him, knowing something like this would happen. "What is it you want from me?" I said with a low growl.

"Calm down, kid! It's nothing to big. I just need you to kill someone for me."

I looked at him like he was out of his damned mind. "I'm sorry. I must have misunderstood you. Did you say you want me to kill someone?"

Zander took a sip of his beer. "Yes, I need you to go to Chinatown and kill Zao. He's a little thieving gremlin that stole from me. I want you to bring me back what he took. Then I will give you the info you were looking for."

I knew I had no choice in the matter because I needed the info. I headed out of the club and made my way to Chinatown. It was a very beautiful culture. I walked around a bit exploring before I got to the job to be done. I found a little shop with a golden dragon above it. Inside were many little statues and other culture products. A little Chinese man was standing behind the counter; he looked to be ancient. "Excuse me, sir, I am looking for someone by the name of Zao!" His eyes grew a bit wider after he heard the name. I could tell he knew whom I was talking about. "I am sorry, but no Zao here!" he replied.

I just nodded and walked out of the shop. I made it about half a block when I found myself surrounded by a group of men. They all looked at me trying to scare me, but it was not working. One of the thugs stepped forward. He looked like he belonged in a Miami Vice episode. "I hear you are looking for Zao… What is it you want from him?" he asked me.

I looked around, inside I was laughing. I could feel my wolf, he wanted blood and I was almost inclined to give it to him. "It doesn't concern you! Do you know where he is?" I said with a commanding tone.

The thug looked behind him making sure his men were still there. Then he turned and smiled at me. "If it concerns Zao, it concerns me… So, I am going to tell you what I think. We are going to have to show you how much it concerns us." In that last word, the gang of men moved, but I moved faster.

It took me less than two seconds to take out the group of them. I left the big mouth alone. He turned and looked at the group that was now lying on their backs. As he looked at me I could smell the fear coming from him. It was so strong it made my wolf and me happy.

"Now tell me where Zao is or I will have to become a bit more insistent about it."

He looked up at me, fear dancing around in his eyes. "He is at the Fortune Cookie down the street."

I walked past him patting the thug on the back. It was not hard to find the Fortune Cookie; it was a tea shop on the corner. I walked in and the smell of different teas clouded my nose. But finding Zao was easy. He was the little guy in the ugly suit running out the back door. I took off after him. The chase enthralled me. I could have caught him at any time. But I slowed up and gave the chase a little bit longer life. We ran three miles before I decided to

55

call this chase to an end. I had him pinned in an alleyway that had only one way out. That way was through me.

This little gremlin reminded me a bit of that awesome actor Danny DeVito. "You have nowhere to run!" I said to him.

He looked around looking like a deer caught in headlights. "Okay, look, you got me. What do you want?"

I walked closer to him breaking the distance between us. "I was sent by the Khan of the weretigers. He said you took something from him and I need that back!" Zao put his hand in his pocket pulling out a coin. It was pure gold and looked to be very old. "Here take it, please, but don't kill me!"

I took the coin placing it in my pocket. Then I looked around and with a bit of energy I grew my claws from my fingers. I took one swipe at the gremlin taking his head off. It bounced off the wall landing next to his now limp body.

I hurried back to the club wanting to get the info that would point me in the direction of Mira. I arrived passing the sweating to the oldies doorman. I found Zander sitting in the corner booth with a stripper on his lap. She was playing with his long hair.

"It's done, here!" I pulled the coin out and tossed it to him.

Zander caught it with his right hand without even taking his eyes off the stripper. "Good job, Liam... now for what I owe you. In the small town of Hollow Falls, Colorado, you will find a woman by the name of Nara. She is the local vet there, and also one of the only immortals to ever be called before the council."

I knew that this was all he was going to tell me. "Thanks and good luck in life," I said as I left the club. It was going to take me a day or two to get to Colorado and I needed to get on the road. As I drove across the Golden Gate Bridge, I noticed how beautiful the city looked. I could now understand what it was that drew people to big cities. The drive was not as peaceful as I would have liked it to be. I started to hear Mira again, she seemed scared and I hated not being there for her.

56

Two days passed and I soon found myself passing by the town sign. It was a work of art. Carvings of the falls and streams showed perfectly. The town was small, almost like Wolf Creek. The only thing missing was the beach. I did not waste any time. I drove to the veterinary hospital. I parked next to a silver Mercedes, it was a beautiful machine. As I opened the door I saw three people waiting with their pets. The receptionist looked at me. She was beautiful.

"Hello," she said to me as I approached the counter.

"I am here to see Nara," I said.

She looked up at me with her dark brown eyes. "Um, do you have an animal that needs to be seen?"

I smiled at her. "No, I do not, but if you can tell her I was sent here to see her by Zander." The receptionist pushed a button on the phone and picked it up to talk.

She said everything I asked her to. I took a seat next to an old lady and her fat orange cat. It kind of reminded me of the doorman in San Francisco. The door to the back opened up and a beautiful Native American woman stepped out. She had on a white lab coat with a grey shirt and tan khakis. She had a necklace around her neck that was nothing but beautiful beads. Her long black hair was kept in a tight braid that ran down her back. She looked at me with her beautiful honey colored eyes. "Please, sir, come with me," she said with a smile that could make any man melt. I followed her through the back and to her office. As I entered, she shut the door and took a seat on the other side of her desk.

"So what can I do for you, child of the moon?"

I looked at her wondering how she knew what I was. "I need your help; I was told by Zander that you could point me in the direction of the council." Her eyes started to form a more focused look to them.

"What do you want with them?" she asked me tapping her finger on the desk.

"They took my charge, the daughter of Vlad Tepes. I am her personal wolfguard and it's my duty to protect her. I need to locate them and get her back!"

She smiled at me but this smile was different, more mischievous. "I highly doubt that the council would take her. I think that Vlad is playing a game with you, boy. Maybe hoping you would try and kill the council and die in the process."

I looked at her and could not tell whether she was lying or not. "That is a risk I must take. Please help me?"

She gazed at me for a minute before she opened a drawer to her desk. She pulled out a stone with the color of blood to it. "Let's go ahead and call the council and see what they have to say." She placed her hands atop the stone closing her eyes. "Deruks, Timelosus, Natrua, Semirosi." The stone begin to glow red and she lifted her hands and a bright red light shot out of it.

"Why do you summon me, Nara?" A vibrating voice asked.

"Forgive me, but I have a question to ask you. Did the council take the daughter of the Vampire Lord?" she asked the mysterious voice.

It went quiet for a second, and then the voice answered. "We, the council, did not take the daughter of Vlad Tepes. We have no reason to take her. Why do you ask?"

I was lost; did Lord Tepes really want me dead?

"I have the wolfguard of the daughter of the vampire lord. He came here telling me that the vampire lord claims you took her!" Nara looked at me smiling.

"He has been fed false information. We had no hand in her abduction." The red light began to fade and soon it was no more.

Nara placed the stone back into her desk. "There you go, the council cannot lie. They are forbidden by the great gods. If he says no, then it is true. They do not have her. If I were you, I would go back and find out what they are trying to do to you!"

58

I was angry and I was on the verge of shifting from the fury inside me.

Nara stood up and walked over to me. She placed her hands on my shoulders. Something happened then. I felt a wash of peace flow over me. "Remember, being a child of the moon can give you great and terrible power. Your Great Mother was one of the most powerful spiritual gods to live."

I got up and then left the veterinary hospital heading back to the vampire lord's home. I wanted answers, and I wanted them now! I pushed my Ducati to the limits trying to make up for lost time on this lie of a quest. It took me three days to reach Washington State, and I soon arrived at the mansion of the lying vampire lord. I burst through the front doors taking a deep breath trying to locate the lying vampire. I followed the scent to his office. He was sitting at his desk, his eyes locked on me the moment he saw me. "YOU LIED TO ME! The council did not have her, so where is she?"

He looked at me his eyes red, fury visible in them. "She is safe, but in order for you to be reunited with her I need you to do something!"

I was pacing back and forth in front of his desk. I was enraged knowing he had her. I wanted what was mine back. "What!"

He rose up from his desk and walked over to the cabinet. He opened it pulling out a book. It was black and bulky. He laid it in front of me opening it. The pages where black with white writing. "This is the text of Blood; I need you to locate an artifact for me. It's the orb of blood tides. Bring this to me, and I will reunite you with Mira!" I felt like he was lying to me once again but I really had no choice.

"Where will I find this orb?" I asked him with a calmer voice.

"In the great mountains of Norway, you will find a small town called Vulkan. The people there protect it."

I looked at his red gaze. "How come you need me to get it? Why can you not get it?" I asked him.

59

"The town is built on holy ground and I am not allowed to pass. Get me what I want and I will set her free." I turned and walked out of the office.

"He left, you can come in now." A small door opened and Mira walked into her father's office.

"Why must we lie to him, father? Why can't I just tell him the truth?" she asked her father while watching Liam leave.

I headed to the docks. I knew I needed to find a boat that sailed to Norway. I found a small charter barge that was heading the way I needed to go. I paid the captain five thousand dollars to take me along with them. It was not easy for me being nowhere near land for a week. I spent the days just watching the crew work. I even helped a bit. But I paid enough so I would not need to work. I stayed as far away from the side of the boat as I could.

We soon arrived at the coastline of Norway. It was beautiful. We docked in a small fishing town from where I had to trek the rest of the way. I made quick time using my werewolf speed to get to the village. I found it nestled deep in the mountain range of the Norwegian Continent.

I walked into this small town that looked like something from the time of westerns and gunslingers. In the middle of the town was a silver statue of a wolf with red eyes.

A man walked up to me in a priest robes. "What brings you to Vulkan, my child?"

I looked at him. His blue eyes looked almost dead. "I have come to collect something," I said to him.

He tapped his finger on his lips. "And what might that be?"

I pointed to the right eye of the statue. "I need the orb from the right eye of the statue."

He stepped back looking at me. "You can never have it. The great goddess Freya bestowed the gem upon our village over a thousand years ago. I must ask you to leave now!"

60

I looked around and the dozen people who lived here were out and surrounding me. "Please father, I do not want to hurt you!"

He looked at me. "It is us who do not want to hurt you, child!"

I stepped back a bit, and in less than a minute I shifted. I stood there now in my wolf form. The villagers stepped away from me, all of them looking at the priest. I turned my yellow gaze upon him.

"You are a son of Freya... We were told a long time ago that one would come to take the orb and stop the demons that drink blood. Please, we do not mean you any harm. If you would, please, show us mercy?"

I turned my head cocking it sideways looking at him. How can I be a child of Freya? I looked around. I was not here to slaughter them. I just wanted the orb. I shifted back and the priest quickly tossed his black jacket around me. "I wish you no harm either. I just want to get the orb and go," I told him.

He placed his arm around me and led me to his church. Once inside he went into the back and brought me one of his priest uniforms. I put it on and took a seat. It has been a very long time since I had been inside any kind of church.

"So, tell me, child of Freya, how can you transform without the power of the moon?"

I looked at the priest. "That is a very long story... but right now I need to take that orb and go!"

The priest got up and started to pace around looking at his pocket watch. Then it hit me, he was holding me for something, killing time. "So tell me priest, who are we waiting for?" I asked him.

He turned and looked at me. I could see the sweat starting to start on his forehead.

"I am sorry, but we were told if one of your kind came here to call."

61

I started to look around. "Call who?!" As I said that, the church doors opened up. In walked a beautiful woman with black skin wearing a red dress and high heels. She had on a fur coat that covered her whole body like a second skin. "Finally, a child of Freya has returned. I have waited for you a long time."

The priest walked over and bowed down before her. She looked down at him placing her hand on his head. "You are a worthy servant, you have pleased me. I grant you and your village everlasting prosperity." The priest rose up from the ground, looked at me and left us alone in the church. This strange woman walked closer to me looking at me with her light blue eyes. "Oh I am terribly sorry. Let me introduce myself. I am Morgana and I am also soon to be your master!" As I backed up from her I could feel the dark energy radiating off of her.

"What do you mean, my master?" I asked.

She walked closer, now only a foot away from me. She took my face into her hands. "I will bond with you binding you to me! With you by my side I will be able to take back my kingdom." I pulled away from her grip on my face. I looked at her wanting to kill her.

She started to chant something but I was not sure what it was. I watched as she pointed to me. I felt a tingle on my skin. She walked over to me once again, kissing me, and then backing away. The look on her face was that of shock. "How can this be?" she hissed.

I was lost. I did not understand what she meant. "You have already been bound to. I cannot complete the bond!" Her voice had a fierce rage to it. She turned pushing the doors open and storming out.

I heard the villagers screaming. I walked out to find the village being set ablaze by Morgana. I knew they had wronged me, but I could not let her destroy this town. I ran shifting my face a bit growing my fangs. I jumped on Morgana digging my fangs in deep, ripping her throat apart. I stood up, her blood dripping to the ground. I felt a bit of satisfaction in her death. The villagers screamed looking at me. I felt as if I did something wrong.

62

The priest walked over to me. "What have you done?!" he said with fear in his voice.

"What do you mean? I saved your homes, I killed the wicked witch."

The priest dropped down on his knees next to the now dead body of Morgana. "Oh, mighty gods, please forgive us. We did not mean harm to your Great Daughter!"

I was lost, but then the sky started to light up, thunder rumbled in the clouds. The villagers started to scream and run, trying to hide from the sky. Lighting started to strike the village. I grabbed the priest hiding under the statue of the wolf. The sky was going crazy and the priest was mumbling under me. Soon rain started to fall out of the sky as if it was weeping for Morgana.

The villagers came out of their homes yelling thanks to the thunderstorm above. "The great gods have spared us," the priest said leaving me alone under the statue.

I climbed out and, while they were busy, I grabbed the orb. I silently walked away from the village. I spent the night walking to the fishing town that I had arrived at. I paid for a room in a small inn next to the wharf. After everything that had happened, I needed some rest. I soon found myself dreaming. I was in a cornfield being circled by crows. I looked around and there was someone standing in front of me, but I could not make out their features.

I reached for this person and they faded away as I touched them. "This is a warning, child of the moon. Do not come back to these lands ever again. If you do, the great gods will kill you!" a voice yelled to me in my dream. I woke to find I was sweating. I looked out the window and saw that it was early morning, maybe 5 am.

I got up and headed to the docks, holding the orb close to me. I found the boat that brought me to Norway. I paid the captain another five thousand to take me back to Seattle, Washington.

Chapter VI: A Dog's Place

I did not go to the vampire lord's manor right away. I headed into town to a local occult store for some info. I looked it up in the yellow pages. It was located on North and 7th. Not too far from the docks, actually. I pulled up to the small shop nestled next to the coffee bean. It had a sign above the door. It read Heaven's Attic, nice name I thought. I opened the door and a small bell started to jingle. "Be with you in a minute," a voice called to me from the back of the shop. I waited by the counter with the orb in a wooden box.

An older man walked out from behind a curtain door. He had on a brown sweater and a pair of pants that looked to belong back in the 60's. He had on a pair of glasses and his long white hair in a ponytail. "What can I do for you kiddo?" he asked me with a smile.

I leaned over the counter looking at some of the stuff in the glass container. "What can you tell me about the Orb of blood tides?"

The old man looked at me for a second and ducked back into the room he came from. When he returned he had a tan book in his hands. He set the book on the counter blowing off the dust on it. "Let me ask you something before I open this book. What does a werewolf want with this orb?"

I was shocked that he knew what I was. "How did you know?" I asked.

He gave a chuckle and opened the book. "I have been in this business for a long time, kid! Now let's see what this orb is used for!" He flipped through the pages stopping about fifteen pages in.

Sure enough, there it was a perfect drawing of the orb. Under it there was writing. I believe it was Latin. "Ok, so it says here that the orb can kill a vampire. Or it can give a vampire the doorway to the nexus. Now the nexus is a supernatural point of energy and with that power a vampire could control the world."

Now I could see why Vlad wanted it, he wanted the power.

64

The old man looked at me with a judging look. "Do you have the orb?" he said with a stern voice. I felt as if it was my father questioning me.

"Yes," I replied.

The old man ducked back into the backroom again, this time staying back there a little bit longer. When he returned he had a box that looked to be made of bronze. "Take this, it will hide the power signature of the orb. No one will be able to feel the energy from it, or even find it wherever you decide to keep it."

"What if I left it with you?" I said placing the wooden box next to the bronze one.

The old man looked at me, then turned his eyes to the wooden box. He opened it slowly making the orb visible. His breathing became heavy and fear washed over him.

"So will you keep it safe for me?"

He looked up at me. "Um, sure, I guess, man, but not for too long," he said pulling the orb out and placing it in the bronze box. I turned and left the shop making my way to the vampire lord's home.

I pulled up on my motorcycle seeing my Impala sitting outside the house. I found Hannibal sitting outside on the stairs smoking a cigar.

He looked up at me and smiled. "Glad to see your still alive, pup! The master is inside."

I did not even say two words to him. I walked into the house finding his personal guards have been upgraded. Instead of human guard servants he had vampires watching his house. I walked into the living room to find the vampire lord sitting on the couch watching the cooking channel. He looked over at me, smiling. I walked around the huge black couch and stood next to the fireplace.

"So did you retrieve what I asked you for?"

65

I looked at him, but he was still watching the cooking channel. "I did, but I am not ready to give it too you yet," I replied.

He reached in grabbing the remote from the end table. He turned the TV off and looked at me. "I am sorry, I thought I heard you tell me you had it but I can't have it."

I took a deep breath, calling on my wolf for strength. "That is because I did!"

In those words he was gone - vanished. I looked around but could not see him.

That all soon changed I felt a tight grip on my throat lifting me from the ground. I looked to find him, eyes as red as blood and fangs showing. "YOU LISTEN HERE, DOG! I AM THE LORD OF ALL THE VAMPIRES. YOU ARE A SERVANT TO MY KIND. NOW GIVE ME THE ORB. IF YOU DO NOT I WILL KILL YOU RIGHT HERE AND NOW!" he yelled.

I knew that he could kill me and I knew I was not strong enough to take him. But I also knew he wanted the orb and he needed me alive. "I don't think I will give it to you just yet. If you want it that bad I would advise you to release me now!" I said to him with a cocky smile on my face.

The vampire lord looked at me, then smiled in return. He released me from his grip dropping me to the floor. As I lay there trying to catch my breath, I looked up to find him gone and back on the couch. He had turned the TV back on. "Well played, pup. Well played!"

I smiled as he said that. I knew I had him and he could do nothing about it. "So tell me what is it you want," he said.

"You know what I want!" I replied.

"Oh, dear, can you please come in here!" I heard a door open and I looked behind him. I found Mira standing in the doorway. She looked untouched by her father. In that moment I knew I had been played. "Hello, Liam, I have missed you."

66

I shook my head, I was now pissed. "So, I see that you were in on your own kidnapping huh!"

Mira looked at me with her violet eyes. "I did not want it to be like this. But I knew if I asked you that you would say no! I am sorry, Liam. I truly am, but we needed that orb. Now please give it to my father so we can go back to our own lives."

I was so angry I began to tremble. The rage was taking me over. Everything in me told me to kill her right then and there. "We are never going to be back to what you want. I am not a play toy for you to toy with. I will not be treated like this!"

Mira looked at me and I could feel her sadness. I had struck her hard with what I said. "This is all entertaining but, dog, you owe me the orb! I reunited you with Mira, now hold up your end of the deal!"

I looked over at him, my eyes burning with a yellow fury. "I want something else! I want you to break my bond with Mira. I want to be free of her!" Mira looked at me and then at her father.

The lord of vampires got up and walked over to the bookcase. He pulled out a book that he opened, inside was a silver knife. "In order to break your bond I will need to take your blood with a silver blade. Then I will cut Mira with it, the silver is a magical essence, it will break the bond." I stuck my arm out looking at Mira. She held herself as if she was cold. "If you do this, Liam, you can never bond with another again," he said placing the knife against my skin.

"I do not care. Do it!" I said. I felt the blade in that moment cutting me, and then he walked over to Mira and stabbed it into her arm. She screamed as he plunged it into her. The energy bond we had faded, I could feel it happening.

I should have felt weaker but for some reason I felt perfectly fine. "Okay, I need to go get it. I have someone holding it for me."

He looked at me smiling. "That is fine, but Hannibal will go with you. After he has it you are free to leave."

67

I nodded and decided to take the Impala this time. I took Hannibal with me. We arrived at the shop but something seemed off.

"I am back for the package," I said as I entered into the shop. I got a response I did not expect.

"Sorry, little wolf, but the orb is not going to that blood sucking bastard." I turned to find a man who looked to be of Japanese descent. He had on a black suit and black jacket. "The council has decided to take an interest in the orb. So that means it's theirs, and there is nothing you can do."

Hannibal pushed past me trying to attack this unknown man. Hannibal dropped to his knees screaming in pain. "Do not try my patience, dog. I am Kai, guardian to the council and I am not easily taken."

I looked over at Hannibal. He now lay motionless on the floor. "What did you do to the shop keeper?" I said demanding to know.

"Do not worry he is safe! If I were you, wolf, I would leave your allegiance to that undead bastard." Kai smiled then in a puff of black smoke he was gone, and so was the orb. I looked down at Hannibal and instead of helping him I just left him there.

I took a quick look through the shop but I did not find the old shopkeeper. I left the shop only to run into a little girl. She had on a red dress with a red bowtie in her hair. Her skin was dark. I thought she was of Mexican descent. She looked up at me with her eyes but she had no color to them. In that moment I could tell she was blind. "Help me up, Duffis!" she said, holding her hand up. I reached down, taking her small hand into mine. She pulled on me helping herself from the ground. She turned her eyes to me, and I could swear she could actually see me.

"So where you heading off to so fast, Wolfy?" she said with a smile.

I was starting to hate that everyone could tell I was a werewolf. "I am sorry for that little girl. I did not mean to run into you."

68

The little girl walked over to me and kicked me in the shin. "Hey what the hell was that for? I said I was sorry," I said looking at her

"Because you ran me over, but I do accept your apology. My name is Isabella, what is yours?"

I tried to study her. There was something about her. She had the taste of magic on her. "My name is Liam Blackmane... now tell me, what are you?"

She giggled, kind of reminding me of Mira. She started to skip around me whistling. "Oh come on, Wolfy, can't you sense what I am?" She walked over taking my hand into hers once again.

I felt a power flowing from her to me, and I had seen something, a giant tree with what I believed was fairies. "Are you one of the fairy kind?"

She looked up at me. "Why, yes I am, Wolfy." She let go of my hand and walked towards the street. Then she disappeared.

I looked around, but sure enough, she was gone. I went back to my car to find Hannibal leaning over it. He was still sore and barely able to keep himself vertical. "What the hell are you doing, pup? Get over here and open the damn door. We need to head back to the mansion." I unlocked the car, and we headed back to Vampire Lord's Manor.

Hannibal burst out of the Impala and stormed inside. I started to follow, but I was soon stopped by Mira. She stood in front of me with sadness on her face. "Liam, I wanted to tell you that I never wanted to hurt you. I love you, and I do not want you to leave me. I need you in my life. An eternity without you is a hell I don't want to go through."

I looked at her and wanted to take her into my arms. But I felt a dark energy blowing towards me from the mansion. I soon had the vampire lord in front of me. His eyes even a darker red then I had ever seen them.

69

"It is because of you, Dog, that I lost the orb to those bastards on the council. As for your bond, I lied - a cut from a silver knife won't break it. All it did was weaken the bond, that is it. You are still my daughter's slave, and you will stay that way until I get what I want!" His voice was not loud, but it radiated power as he talked. I could only bow before him. "Master, I am sorry I failed you!" I lifted my head and saw Hannibal kneeling before his master.

The vampire lord looked at Hannibal taking his broad shoulder and helping him to his feet. "I do not blame you, my faithful servant. Kai is a powerful wizard; he is not someone to trifle with. I applaud your courage to even try and take him. This is why you are my personal wolfguard." I could have sworn I could see an invisible tail connected to Hannibal wagging. He was like an obedient housedog. The vampire lord turned his eyes back to me. "Go get me my orb back or I will kill you." I just bowed and walked away leaving Mira with her father.

As I walked out of the mansion my pendant started to glow. My sister stood before me. "Please listen to me, I was on the other side. The spirits are talking and they have heard that the blood drinkers will kill you once they have what they want." Celeste looked at me with her saddened ghost eyes.

"I figured that, did you hear anything about Mira?" I asked her.

Celeste dropped her head. "He is going to kill her also. Mira broke their most sacred law; she fell in love with her wolfguard. Her life has been forfeited." I took a deep breath and Celeste vanished.

I left the Impala and got on my motorcycle. I did not want anything from them, that included the car. I took off not even sure where I was going to start to look for the council. I rode back into town stopping at the only place I knew to go. I went back to the occult store. I walked in and found the old man alive and well. "Where have you been? And how the hell did the council find out you have the orb. You told me that the box would shield it from anyone!" he looked at me placing his finger to his mouth.

"Come with me to the back," he said.

I looked around first, and then I followed him. We walked into a back room with a black door. Inside the room were symbols all over the walls and floors, even the ceiling. In the middle of the room was a séance table.

"I wanted to apologize to you about what happened. I was wrong. I guess that bronze box was not as powerful as I thought it was. This room will keep everything we talk about from getting to the council. I have known Kai for a very long time. He was the one who got me started in the occult culture. After you left me the orb, he just appeared. It was the first time I had seen him in over twenty years. He was still as young as the last time I saw him. He told me that the orb was too dangerous for me to have, and he needed to take it from me. I was not going to doubt him, so I gave it to him." The old man sat down placing his hands on the table.

"I need your help. I need to find the council or the one I love will die. Please help me!" I said. He raised his head up and looked at me. I could see fear in his eyes.

"I do not know where they are, but I think we can summon Kai here!" The old man quickly got up and went out into the front. I heard him rattling around in there and then he came back in to the room. He had a ton of herbs and stuff in his arms. He set a golden bowl in the middle of the table. I watched him place many different items into the bowl. Then he cut his hand dropping blood into it last.

He started to mumble something and then the bowl started to smoke. A flame shot out of it and standing on the other side of the table was Kai. He looked around while fixing his expensive black jacket. "Why did you summon me here?" he asked.

The old man said nothing so I figured it was my turn. "You took something from me and I want it back."

Kai just looked at his finger nails pretty much ignoring me.

"I need it back Kai… He has Mira and he is going to kill me and her if he does not get it."

71

Kai turned and looked at the old man. "Hey Jimmy, can you give us a few minutes in private, please." The old man looked at me, and then back to Kai. He turned and left Kai and me alone in the room.

Kai walked around touching the walls making the symbols glow. "Listen up, wolf, if you want that orb back you will have to take it up with the elders. One of the elders lives here in Washington next to a town called Forks. He has been here for a very long time and he is not one who likes to be bothered." Kai pulled out a card, handed to me, and vanished. The symbols stopped glowing as he left.

I looked at the address on the card, and then left the room without saying anything to the old man. I got on my motorcycle and left. The address was in a small town called Bright Harbor. I drove through the harbor town. It was almost Eden, like I felt a wave of peace hit me as I passed the town sign. I arrived at the address on the card. It was a small one story white house. It looked like something out of a fairy tale. Before I could open the gate I was standing before a man. He was built with a ton of muscles and was at least seven foot in height. His hair was black and his beard ran down his chest. What stuck out the most were his eyes. They had a tint of green and red mixed in them. "What are you doing in my town, werewolf?" I was not even sure why but I was scared of him and so was my wolf.

"Kai gave me your address. He said you are an Elder. I need the orb back you took from me!" He looked at me shaking his head as if I was doing something wrong. "Do you know who I am?"

I had no idea who or what he was. "No sir!" I said trying to act a bit tough. "I am Anoki, great spirit god of fire and your great mother's brother. I, unlike her, have lived my eternal life serving the humans of the world. I joined the council to keep this planet safe. If you take that orb to Vlad, I do not even think the council could stop him. Vlad was the only child of the spirit of the night, Dakaria, my brother. After Dakaria found out Vlad was born, he left the mortal world leaving his legacy to Vlad. When that blood-sucking demon was born, he was infused with great power. This kind of power should have never been given to him. But Dakaria

72

was a demented spirit and cared nothing for us or any of the mortals of this world." I could hear the truth coming from Anoki. He was sincere in everything he was saying.

"Hey Mister Belmont, how is your day going?" I turned to see a young boy who could have been my age. I noticed he was waving to Anoki as he drove by.

"Belmont huh…" I said to him turning back around.

He shrugged his huge shoulders. "I am the local history teacher here. I let myself age in order to stay in the town. After fifty years I faked my death and changed my features. I have lived in this town for over three hundred years. Listen to me carefully, child of the moon. I cannot give you back the orb. But I may be able to help you."

He looked at me and smiled, but it was hard to see through his bushed beard. "How can you do that?" I asked him.

He pulled a red gem from his pant pocket. He closed his hand around it and a bright red light started to glow. His hand looked like a bright red light. The light started to disappear and he opened his hand. Inside was the blood tide orb. "I thought you said I could not take that to him?" I said.

Anoki looked down at the newly created orb and tossed it at me. I caught it and he just laughed. "That is just a knock off I made from a ruby. It has the same magical essence that the orb did. It will hold the shape of the orb for a week but after that it will revert. That should give you enough time to get your love and leave. Good luck, pup."

He turned and walked back into his house. I stood there looking down at the orb, and then my cellphone rang. "Hello," I answered.

"Liam, it's me, Nyssa. I need your help." She sounded panicky and out of breath.

"What's wrong?" I listened to her, she sounded like she was running. "They are after me. I need your help. The pack is all dead. I am the only one who escaped." The phone went dead and she was

73

no longer there. I looked at the orb again and I had to make a choice to either save Mira, or save Nyssa.

I was not sure what to do. I loved Mira but I also loved Nyssa just as much. I dropped the orb on the ground jumping on my motorcycle and started to head to Wolf Creek. I knew what I had to do and I hoped that I was right about Mira's dad not killing her right away. It took me four days to get back to Wolf Creek. I rolled through town and noticed the bar was burned down and no longer there. The streets were silent, not a soul on them. It was eerie, not something you see in a town like this. Last time I was here it was pretty busy, even had a few tourists in it. I pushed through looking around trying to find Nyssa. The night air brought scents of vampires, and there were many different ones.

I took in a deep smell and picked up Nyssa's scent. I followed it like a bloodhound. I ended up at the cottage. The scent ended. I opened the door to find the living room destroyed. Claw marks all along the walls. It looked like a war went down in here. "NYSSA, ARE YOU HERE?" I yelled walking through the house. I turned to a noise coming from the master bedroom. I opened the door nice and slow. I poked my head in looking around while pushing the door all the way open. Next thing I knew I had a giant wolf on me, growling. I looked at the wolf; it was Nyssa. Soon it went from growls to whining. She buried her face into mine. I could hear her heart; it was racing.

I pushed her off and she sat down looking at me. In this form I could not understand her so I had to make due. I stayed with her until night turned to day and she was back in her human form. I quickly located her some clothes to put on. As much as I enjoyed seeing her perfect body, I knew she was uncomfortable. Nyssa came out of the bathroom. She was still flushed from the shift. It takes a lot of energy out of a werewolf during the shift.

"So what the hell is going on here?" I asked Nyssa while pouring her some water.

She downed it in a matter of moments. "I have been running from these blood suckers for two weeks. They came in and just went to work on destroying the town. We killed many of them, but

74

in the end the pack was wiped out, even my brother. I decided to run instead of trying to kill them after they dismembered the pack." She was still scared.

"Do you know why they came here?" I asked her. As she looked at me I knew she did not have a clue. "We need to leave town, there is nothing here anymore." I pulled Nyssa out of the house with me. That was mistake number one. The vampire goon squad was outside waiting for us. I pushed her behind me blocking her from the vampires with my body. "What are you doing here?" I said to the vampires. They just glared at me like confused teenagers after the prom.

One vampire pushed his way through the crowd. He had on a charcoal black pinstriped suit. His long red hair ran down to his butt. He walked with grace and power. I knew he was the leader of the bunch. "Well, if it's not the personal wolfguard of the Princess. What are you doing here?" he said, licking his fangs.

"That is not the question you should be asking yourself. You should be wondering which one of you I am going to kill first." He looked around and then started to laugh. The group started to laugh with him. I pushed Nyssa back into the house shutting the door. After I knew she was safe, I started to shift but just enough to bring out my wolf. I went at them knocking the leader to the ground. I pushed past him, slicing my way through the bunch cutting their heads off. Soon I stood with a pile of dead vampire bodies at my feet.

The one I let live - the leader – then stood up looking around. I could see his red eyes growing as he saw his friends dead. He lifted his gaze to me. The fear flowed off of him like cologne. He charged me, as he did I shot my right hand through his chest, tearing out his heart. His limp body hung on my arm. I released his heart, pulling my arm clear of his chest. He fell, now joining the rest of the dead bodies. I went back inside and grabbed Nyssa, leaving the town.

Chapter VII: Friend or Foe

I decided it was not safe to take Nyssa with me. I took her to the airport in Rockland, sending her to the only place I knew she would be safe. Back home to Wasilla, Alaska. I knew she would be safe back at my parents' home. She did not want to go, of course, but I could not bear her getting hurt. I left Rockland and started my long drive back to Seattle, Washington. The entire ride back I could not stop thinking about how I betrayed Mira. It was hard for me. I could no longer feel Mira; the bond was truly weakened. I felt kind of naked not being able to feel her, and it was hard for me to accept.

I hit Washington. It was a bad ride, as the rain was pouring fast and hard. These are the times I missed owning a car. I made it to Seattle and I decided to spend the night here to rest for what is to come. I found a Motel 9 located down by the docks. It was not too shabby for a no-star hotel. I sat by my motel window listening to the ocean, it was peaceful. I knew that I had to soon face an advisory that was out of my league. But I knew I needed to pull it together and do what needed to be done. As soon as I started to relax, I heard a knock at my room door. I got up slowly setting my glass of water on the table. By the scent, whoever was there was not human. I opened the door slowly to find Isabella standing there. "Well, are you going to let me in, knucklehead?" she asked with a smile.

I opened the door a bit, and she strolled in taking a seat by the window. I closed the door and looked at her. "What brings you to my motel room?"

She looked at me and the happiness dropped from her face. "I was forbidden to come here, but I had to. A great war is coming, and the council is looking to you. They believe that you are the one prophesied to come and kill the dark lord vampire Vlad. I know you have great power, but I do not believe you are ready to take him on. He was once a member of the council, before he let the power consume him."

I was not sure why she was telling me this. "Why is the council so scared of him?" I asked her.

She turned her head looking out at the docks. "Because Vlad commands the allegiances of most of the supernatural houses. If they decided to take him, they would have to face the army he controls. So it is up to you to make sure that never happens. We need you, Liam. We need you to save us from his dark hands." I could see the tears running down her childlike face. Before I could say anything, a bright white light flashed and she was gone.

I tried to sleep but I had way too much on my mind. I felt like it was in overdrive and my brain would not shut off. I must have been lying in the bed for hours until I finally dozed off.

I could not tell you how long I slept but it did not seem like long. Soon the sun was rising and night was disappearing. I got up out of the rock hard bed, my back was killing me. I took a nice cold shower, since the hot water was nonexistent. I got dressed and headed out back to the den of the monster. I found over a dozen cars parked outside the mansion, it was packed. I parked my motorcycle by the Impala. I took my helmet off to find four vampire guards surrounding me.

"Hey guys, long time no see huh!" I said with a smile. The guards did not say anything to me, they just stared at me.

"Easy, guys, let's not scare off the wolfguard." I looked around one of the guards to see Franklyn. He was the cousin to Mira and I had only met him only one time before today. He had on tan Dockers, a white shirt, and some DC shoes. His hair was white and short, and he had eyes the color of violet like Mira. The guards bowed to him, making a path so he could walk to me. "How have you been, Liam?"

I was not sure if he was putting on a show or was genuinely asking. "Eh… Could be better but that's life, right? So what is it I have in store for myself?" I asked him.

Franklyn smiled at me. "I am not the one judging you. Only the lord can tell you what is going to happen. But I do need you to follow me inside and let's get this party started."

I knew I had no choice and I knew I had to find Mira to make sure she was ok. I followed Franklyn back into the mansion slowly

77

and cautiously. It was packed with guards - some vampires, some humans and some werewolves. We went into the meeting hall in the back of the house. There was a long brown table with four vampires sitting at it. At the head of the table was the lord vampire Vlad. As for the others I had no idea who they were but I could feel the power flowing from them. Franklyn left my side taking a stance next to the vampire lord. "Welcome home, dog!" the vampire lord said.

"Yeah whatever, let's get on with it. Where is Mira? What have you done to her?" I asked with a growl in my voice. He looked at me, his eyes a deep red. I could tell he just fed not too long ago.

"Mira, darling, can you please come in here?" He said. A door on the side of the room opened and Mira strolled in. She had on a long black gown with her hair up in a ponytail. She looked amazing to me and my heart started to beat faster.

"Mira are you okay?" I asked her.

She barely looked at me. She walked over standing on the other side by her father and Franklyn.

"Look, darling, your lost wolf has found his way home. Are you happy to see him?" he asked her.

She placed her right hand on his shoulder. "Yes, father, I missed him," she replied.

I was lost, I could not tell if she missed me or not. I was for the first time unsure of myself with her. I tried to look at her and get her to look back at me. But it was as if she was oblivious to me being in the room. "So, now the question is what to do with you?" I stood my ground waiting for whatever he decided.

Then a great rage of fire shot up from the floor and standing in front of me was Kai and Anoki. The vampire lord's eyes soon went from pleasing looks to hatred. "What brings you to my home?"

Anoki looked back at me and winked. "Oh, Vlad, you have been missed. But I come here as your dearest friend, and also a council member. I am here to inform you that this wolf here is off

78

limits to you. He has been picked as a chosen one and that means he is untouchable. We are going to take him. I advise you to not make any drastic moves against us!"

The vampire lord started to laugh. "Go ahead, brother, take the dog with you. I was going to have to kill him anyways. Oh, and can you please give Teagan my best, please? I do miss him so."

Anoki turned placing his hand on my shoulder and I felt a surge of energy hit me. I soon found myself in a room made out of marble. It was weird. There was a cloud like substance rolling on the floor. I bent over trying to breathe again. I was unaccustomed to the travel of teleportation. "Where are we?" I asked taking deep breathes.

Anoki looked back at me as Kai walked away. "This is the arch, a sacred realm that we of the council created. It is a place of solace and peace for us. I brought you here to keep you safe until you are ready to take on Vlad."

I looked around and I hated not knowing exactly where this place was. I soon stopped, finding myself looking at what I could only see as an angel. He was beautiful, covered in armor with tan skin and giant red wings. His hair matched his wings. "Welcome to sanctuary, young werewolf. I am Teagan, great god of time and space." I looked over at Anoki he was on one knee bowing before this Teagan god.

"Are you an angel?" I asked him like a dummy.

He laughed and it echoed through the marble room. "In another time my kind were called angels, yes, but I am an Ancronian, one of the very few of my kind that are left," he replied with a perfect smile.

Anoki got up and walked over, taking Teagan's hand in a handshake. They both smiled then looked at me. "Teagan, this young wolf is the one foretold who would kill Vlad." Teagan just smiled and placed his arm around Anoki as they walked away from me. I could hear them whispering but it was weird. It was as if my werewolf hearing was blocked and I could not hear them.

79

They talked for a bit, Teagan left and Anoki turned making his way back over to me. "Well, Liam, it is time to take you to a place you can learn to control your full power and be safe." I was not sure what he meant. Anoki bent down placing his finger in the middle of my forehead. I started to feel that same energy flowing into me again. I found myself no longer standing in the marble room, but in a wooded area with a small town nestled in it.

I found Anoki standing next to me. I followed him as he walked towards the town that was close by. It was nothing like I had ever seen before. It looked so old, like something you would see in a medieval movie. Then I noticed I was no longer in my own timeline, I was in the past. "Where are we at Anoki?" I said still looking around. He just smiled at me as we walked past the iron forges. I stopped, watching the blacksmith beat on a long peace of bronze steel.

"I brought you here so you can learn to become a real werewolf. Here you will be trained and learn to harness the power inside you."

We stopped walking standing outside a giant house. The front door opened and a tall man with tan skin, long white hair and blue eyes stepped out. He was powerful; I could feel his essence hitting me like a tidal wave.

"Long time no see, Dante!" Anoki said to him. Dante stuck out his large hand, taking Anoki's hand in friendship.

"Are you from this timeline?" Dante asked.

Anoki just smiled at him. "No, we are not. I need you to watch over this pup here. I want you to train him and show him the great power of the wolf. He is our chosen one and we need him." Anoki burst into flames and vanished.

I now stood next to a man I never should have met. I was not in my own time and I was not sure what I could expect. "Well, come inside and let's have a chat while we eat dinner." I followed him inside, it was weird. I was not used to not having electricity and having to rely on candles. We walked down the hall into the kitchen. There was a beautiful blonde headed woman cooking. She

80

had on a light red dress with a tan trim on it. "Olympia, we have company." She turned; her face was almost too perfect. I could not see a flaw in it. She looked almost unreal to me. But something soon caught me, it was her scent. It smelled like the scent of Isabella, the fairy. Was she one of them I thought to myself?

I looked over to Dante as he sat down at the table. "Um, is she, well, one of the fairy kind?" I asked him taking a seat at the table.

Dante started to laugh. "My boy, you are very young aren't you? Yes, Olympia is a forest Fairy and she is also my wife. Do not worry. I am going to teach you the right way to live like a werewolf!" Olympia walked back and smiled at me setting a huge plate of food in front of me. It has been such a long time since I had a home cooked meal. We ate dinner in peace, no one said a word. It was actually nice. Dante finished his food quite quickly. I was barely through half of my plate.

"Well, let's go start that wolf training of yours, pup!" He said standing up and stretching. I took one last bite and followed him out of the house. We stood outside as the day was coming to an end. "What do you hear?" he asked me.

I was not sure what he meant by that. "I do not understand what you mean," I said, looking up at him. He was at least five inches taller than I was.

He had his eyes closed and head tilted as if he was looking up at the sky. "Just close your eyes and listen, take in everything around you." The night air was sweet and I have never smelt such clean air. Pollution was not a problem in this time.

I closed my eyes and joined in with Dante, trying to do as he asked me too. I started to hear hoofs running on the ground. People chattering about wild boars being in the forest. I was not sure what he wanted me to listen for. "I can't do this; I do not understand. I only hear the villagers and the local sounds." Dante just made a hushing sound to me. I closed my eyes again and tried ever harder. I started to block out the local sounds of the village trying to hear everything that was not around me. Just when I was about to give up I heard the sound of a stream. It sounded like it was right by

81

me. Then I heard the sound of animals in the forest scurrying around in the darkness.

I opened my eyes to find Dante gone. I started to look around trying to find him. "Concentrate on my voice. You may not be able to see me but you can find me if you listen to my voice!" I closed my eyes and started to try and locate Dante. First step was to get rid of the sounds I did not want. I concentrated and soon the sounds of the village vanished again. Now I needed to find Dante. I let my sense of hearing become my new eyes. I started to see in a new way, it was like using my eyes but I could see everywhere. I found Dante. He was sitting on a tree stump waiting for me. I opened my eyes and headed to him. He looked up at me with his cool blue eyes. "You are a natural, kid. That little trick is called 'Third Sight.' We can use our hearing to take on the form of seeing."

Dante got up and we headed out in the forest. The moon was hanging in the night sky. It was not full, but it was beautiful. We stopped at the stream. I heard it was just like I had pictured it. Dante looked down at the stream and then started to strip.

"WOOO, buddy! I do not think I want to take part in any of this training," I said averting my eyes from him. I expected him to make a response but he said nothing. I turned back around and standing by me was a dark chocolate colored wolf. "How the hell did you shift, without the full moon?" I said to the wolf. He just bobbed his head at me. I stripped and made the shift. Before I knew it I felt his teeth bite into my fur. He tossed me across the stream just looking at me with his yellow eyes.

I pulled myself off the ground shaking it off and he was on me again. He rammed into me with his much defined wolf body. I rolled across the ground the pain was bad. I had never been hit that hard. "Do something or I am going to kill you!" I looked at him not sure how he could talk to me. "I am using my newly created wolf mind. In wolf form you can talk to other wolves, with just a thought," he said to me as he howled to the moon. I got up and charged at him trying to grab him but he was faster. Dante moved out of the way grabbing me and slinging me across the stream. I smashed into a huge oak tree and I was knocked out.

When I awoke I was back in Dante's house and in human form. I was lying in a bed made of feathers and straw. I soon found I was not wearing my own clothes. I had on some kind of robes and shirts made of dark blue and gold colors. My necklace was missing and I could not feel my sister anymore. I climbed out of the make shift bed and headed down the stairs. I found that it was morning. I must have been out all night. Dante was sitting at the table eating bread and some type of soup. He looked up at me. "Well, we got a long day lad, come eat." I took the same seat next to him and Olympia sat on the other side.

"Hey, did you guys notice what happen to my necklace?"

Dante looked over at Olympia "Well, dear, did you do anything with his necklace?" he asked her.

She looked up at me. I started to feel very embarrassed. "I am sorry, love, you had no necklace on since you have been here. I did not see you with any necklace on the night you came here with the fire spirit."

I started to try and remember where it could have gone. I tried to finish my food before Dante this time. But he beat me to it. He got up and looked at me. I started to feel like he was my alpha, my leader. "Thank you for the food, Olympia," I said running out the door behind Dante.

I followed Dante out to the forge where he stopped and inspected a few weapons. "Good job, Kyle, really good," he said to the blacksmith. I started to see that Dante was a very important man in the village. We hit up a couple dozen more little shops before we headed over to the stables. The horses started to freak out kicking and whining. All creatures get scared once we come near them. The wolf inside of us makes us predators to all wildlife. "Pay attention, lad. Please step back away from the horses." I took a few steps back while Dante stayed close to them.

I watched him take a deep breath and something changed. I could no longer feel his power; it was as if he was just human. The horses stopped freaking out and Dante walked over and touched them. They made no more noises as he petted them.

83

"How did you do that?" I asked him.

Dante walked back over to me letting his inner wolf free again. "You can learn to quiet your brother, the wolf. This is called the shadow bind. It makes the wolf sleep and makes you seem human. In this it allows you to get around without being felt or even smelled out. This is a trick I will teach you soon enough. As for today, you and I have to meet up with a friend of mine." He looked at me and then took off.

I opened my connection to my wolf and used his great speed. I found myself keeping up with Dante. It was not easy but I did it. We ran through the great forest. It was nice and felt good to run again with another werewolf. I stopped as soon as I picked up the scent of a witch. Dante stopped also

"Why are we here?" I asked him.

He looked back at me, his eyes still cool with the color yellow. "I need to make sure the council is right about you." We walked the rest of the way coming to a house made of stone and straw.

It looked like a hut and smelled of mud and cherries. "Kiana!" Dante yelled. The fragile looking door opened up and an old woman walked out. She had on tattered robes. She had grey hair that looked to have never been combed.

She looked at me and then at Dante. "Well, Dante, what brings you and this new wolf to my home?" she said sounding like the witch from Oz.

"Anoki brought him from the future. Told me he is the chosen one. I wanted you to tell me if it's true or not."

She walked slowly over to me, I was stiffening up. I was kind of scared, not sure what she was going to do to me. "Relax, little future wolf, I will not hurt you," she said stopping and looking up at me.

She reached up touching my face with her dirty hands. She closed her eyes and started to breathe harder. I felt a tingle in my face. I could feel the magic flow over my entire body. I started to

84

glow a bright yellow color. It lasted only moments before it faded then she let go of me and smiled. "See, I told you I would not hurt you. Dante, he is the one who will bring an end to the vampires' master. He is the chosen one, you must keep him safe at all cost." Dante smiled and walked over to me.

"I, Dante Bloodmoore, hereby swear my loyalty to you and pledge to protect you until my death."

I stood there, unable to understand why he was doing this. What does it really mean to be the chosen one? How the hell am I going to ever get the power to kill the vampire lord? Dante thanked the witch with some gold and we left. The whole way back I said nothing to Dante. I was still not sure how to act. We arrived back at the village to find the villagers rounded up. There was a garrison of knights in the small village now. "What is going on here?" Dante asked one of the knights.

"My apologies, Sir Bloodmoore, but we have reason to believe that there is a monster in this village. One of your villagers came to the king's court pleading with us to help. So here we are. Let us find this monster and kill it."

Dante nodded for me to go inside the house with Olympia. He stayed outside and did the check with the knights. Hours passed and he finally returned. "They are leaving now. I assured them that they were given false information. For now, we are safe. I do believe it is time that we leave this place though."

I watched Olympia nod to Dante, she agreed with him. That night I helped them pack up the house and put everything on the wagon behind the horse. We left the village behind without saying anything to anyone.

Chapter VIII: New Hope

We did not stop once through the night. Dante was like a machine. He never swayed once showing he was tired. Olympia stayed by his side the whole night, as for me, I crashed in the back of the wagon. When I awoke we had stopped next to a beautiful waterfall. I rose up from the wagon to find Olympia naked, washing up in the waterfall. I wanted to turn my head, but it was as if something was holding my gaze upon her.

"She is beautiful, is she not?"

I shook my head to find Dante standing next to the wagon. "Um, yes she is...I apologize. I did not mean to stare at her like that."

Dante just looked at me and slapped my back. "Do not fret, my young lad. It was not you. She has the lust effect on all men. Except for me, it seemed I was unaffected by her. This is why she had chosen me to be her eternal mate."

I looked again and she was no longer in the falls. "Where did she go?" I asked Dante.

"This is her realm, she is out talking with nature. She will be back in a while. Let's eat while we wait for her, shall we?"

I climbed out of the wagon and took a seat next to Dante on the ground. The sunlight hit all around the forest like lasers. Dante pulled out some day old meat tossing me a few pieces. "We will arrive at our new home tonight," he said ripping a piece of the meat off with his sharp teeth. I ate what he had given me. It was a little bland but a fed wolf was much better than a hungry one.

"How long have you been a werewolf, Dante?" I asked him while chewing my meat.

"A very long time, I was born in the time of gods. I was once a slave born to battle as a gladiator. I battled for the amusement of one man, the great Emperor of Rome. My first fight was with a fierce and very skilled warrior. His name was Sether, the reaper of death. I stood my ground not backing down from him. I figured me

86

being a slave and never a warrior like him, I would surely die. But the gods were on my side this day, and I struck with my short blade taking his head from his shoulders. The great crowed roared chanting my name, as I was the victor of the match. That night, my master praised me for my battle. He supplied me with women and rum the whole night. I awoke twisted with women all around me and my cell door opening. It was one of the guards. He called for the females to leave, and I was soon alone. The guard seemed to be very angry for some reason. He walked over to me, pulling his blade and stabbing me in the chest. I died that night. When I awoke I found myself lying covered in blood in a field. I thought to myself I was in Elysium. That was the day I became more than human. I became a werewolf," he said eating his last piece of meat. Dante stood up stretching his legs. "Olympia, my love, it is time we move along," he said into the woods.

A great gust of wind blew, and Olympia appeared, wearing a dark green dress. "I am here."

Dante looked at me. I got up from the ground and climbed back into the wagon. We spent the next couple of hours traveling until we came to an even larger house than the previous one. It was beautiful. The wood was carved and twisted in unbelievable ways. I felt like it was from a fairy tale I was stuck in. "Dante, this home of yours is amazing!" I said climbing out of the wagon.

"It was a gift from the master wood workers, the elves of the forest," he replied taking Olympia's hand and helping her down.

The doors opened and three gnomes scurried out bowing to Olympia and Dante. They looked just like the fake garden gnomes back home. They came to the wagon unloading it with magic. Olympia went inside and Dante took me around the house. There was a huge garden like the one next to the vampire lord's mansion. I could see more gnomes in the garden tending to it. "These great creatures are the children of my wife Olympia. She created them all to help take care of our home and us. She calls them gnomes. I find them a bit weird, to tell you the truth. Let's take a walk. I want to show you something."

87

I followed Dante into the forest behind the house. It was a peaceful and breathtaking walk. It kind of reminded me of home a bit. I started to miss Alaska, and I started to think about Nyssa. I was lost in thought and found myself running into Dante. It was like hitting a brick wall. "Sorry - was not looking where I was going." I looked around Dante to see a great altar made of marble. I looked harder and there was a statue that looked just like Anoki.

"I first met Anoki when I escaped Rome and made my way back to Greece. It was the night of my first full moon. I shifted and killed an entire village. When I awoke the next morning, I had blood all over my naked body. I found dead bodies all around me and I was scared. Then Anoki appeared before me. He reached down and took my hand into his. As he touched me clothes appeared on me. At first, I took him for a god but I was soon corrected. Many considered him to be a god. But he hated being compared to them. He called them soulless beings who cared nothing for mankind. He also likes to remind me and everyone else that he was much older than them. I spent a few years with Anoki. He became a good friend to me." Dante walked over and lit the golden bowl that sat by the statue of Anoki. A great fire burned with blue flames.

Dante walked away from the altar, and we just watched the flame burn. "I lit it to signal to Anoki that we are here. So when he decides to come for you he will know where we are. This place is magically protected. Let's head back to the house, shall we?" We ran back to the house.

Olympia and two female gnomes were cooking in the massive kitchen. Dante walked over and kissed Olympia softly on her neck before stealing a carrot from the counter. He laughed as Olympia slapped his hand. "Liam, please come with me while the lady of the house and her children prepare our meal."

I followed him up the spiral stairs to the second floor. There were four rooms upstairs. We stopped outside the last door at the end of the hall. Dante stood there. I could feel something but I was not sure what it was. He opened the door and the room was made of silver and in the middle of the room was a giant silver cage. The most shocking part of the room was the giant blood red wolf

88

locked inside the cage. The wolf stood up and let out a vicious roar. "This is my son, Kaliban. On his twentieth birthday he shifted and was never able to take human form again. He is a beast, no more humanity inside him. I have tried to link minds with him, but it has not worked. Olympia believes that he is like this because our two bloodlines are not supposed to mix."

There was something about Kaliban that called to me. I pushed passed Dante and walked closer to the cage.

"Stop, do not move any closer to him!" Dante yelled.

I stopped just as he asked me to. I stood there staring the unstable wolf in the eyes. "Let's go!" Dante said as he grabbed my shoulder. I turned and we left the room. Dante closed it placing his hand in the middle of the door. We went back down stairs. The smell of the food was calling to me. We needed to eat for the full moon was tonight. We sat at the large wooden table and in the middle was a carving of a giant tree.

"What is with the carved tree in the table?" I asked Dante.

"That is my home." I turned my head, it was Olympia answering. I was caught off guard. This was the first time she talked to me.

"Well, it looks to be a beautiful place indeed," I replied with a smile. The gnomes placed the food on the table and then left us to eat. We waited to let Olympia make her plate before we took our food. Two werewolves meant there would not be that much food left. The more energy we could build up before tonight would make the shift easier for us. We dug in and between the both of us there was nothing left. I leaned back in the wood chair resting. I was so full if I had a button on my pants I would have had to undo it.

I got up. I could already feel the moon calling to me. I looked over at Dante, and he was just sitting and relaxing still. "Should we head out, Dante?" I said, breathing a bit harder than usual.

"Yes, let us go for the night. My great flower, I will return to you in the morning. I love you," he said leaning in to kiss

89

Olympia's forehead. We walked out front stripping down, letting the moonlight fill us with energy. I started to shift. I was not sure who shifted faster, Dante or me. But when I was done so was Dante. I followed Dante into the forest, letting my newly formed senses take over.

The moon called to us like mothers to their children. We ran miles, going deeper and deeper into the forest. Our run soon came to a halt. Dante stopped sticking his muzzle into the air. "Vampires - and they are close. I hope you are ready, lad," he said to me taking off in the direction of the vampire scent.

Dante slowed up as we came near them. He used the shadow trick to hide himself. "It is time for you to learn more. Concentrate on hiding yourself, push your wolf back and take complete control of yourself."

I did as he told me, pushing my wolf away not letting him control anything in the hunt. I could feel the change. It was weird, very weird, but I did it. Dante and I got close to the vampire camp. They did not even notice us getting near them.

"We are going to kill them. They are in my territory and I won't tolerate that. Let your wolf lose!" I felt Dante once again he burst out of the tree line attacking the first vampire in his sight. I let my wolf lose again and followed, taking the vampire who was charging at him.

The vampire blood gushed with every bite I took. His screams echoed in the night. I enjoyed killing them. Dante was already on the last vampire, ripping his flesh from his bones. I dropped the now dead vampire and looked over at Dante. I had never felt the power that Dante was releasing as he finished off the vampire. We stood there standing over three vampire bodies.

"Not too bad, not too bad at all, Liam," Dante said walking passed me. I turned and Dante took off fast. I was not sure what was going on but I took off trying to keep up with him. But his speed was amazing. I could barely keep him in my sight. I picked up the smell of smoke coming from the direction of the house. As the forest started to thin I stopped behind Dante. His house was on fire. We watched as the gnomes disappeared into the forest. Dante took off and hit the door hard causing it to shatter like glass.

I waited for him. I wanted to go in but the fire was something I did not want. It could kill a werewolf. I heard a cracking sound and saw Dante jumping out of the top floor window with Olympia on his back. He brought her over to me laying her on her back on the cool grass. I could hear her she was breathing she was still alive. "What about Kaliban?" I asked Dante.

He looked up at the house. "Whoever did this let him free. I am sorry, lad, but I need to take care of my own. I can no longer train you," he said to me. I felt a sadness come over me like he was abandoning me.

I took off, leaving him with Olympia. I headed to the altar of Anoki. I wanted to go back to my time. I sat there looking up at the statue of Anoki. "If you can hear me, I want to go back now. I want to go to my own time!" I said using my mind. He did not respond to me. I just stayed there at the altar the rest of the night.

The morning light woke me up. I was still lying next to the altar. "So you are ready to go home?" I turned my head and Anoki was sitting there.

"Yes I am…Dante said he can no longer train me. So there is no point in staying in this time!" I said to him with a growl.

Anoki walked over to me and touched my shoulder. "Well then let's go shall we?" Again the energy came over me and I felt something pulling me. The energy faded and I was standing next to Anoki. We were back next to his altar but it was covered in ivy and plants.

"Are we back in my own time?" I asked him.

"Well not exactly, I wanted to show you one more thing before I take you back."

I followed Anoki through the trees to come upon a clearing. It was a cliff face covered in green grass. Anoki stood at the edge of

91

it. I walked over to join him. I looked out at a city that was in ruins.

"What happened here?" I asked him.

"This is what's left of San Francisco after the plague of the vampire swept through it. If Vlad is not stopped this is what awaits the entire world. He will bring death to everything he touches."

Anoki looked at me as he grabbed my arm. Soon I opened my eyes and we were outside my house in Wasilla, Alaska. "Thank you for bringing me back home," I said turning to find Anoki gone. I looked over to the front door of the house to find Nyssa looking at me.

My heart started to beat faster as she ran towards me, tackling me to the ground. "I thought you died. I am so glad you are home," she said holding me tight. I rose up from the ground, holding her body against mine. I carried her into the house. Her breath on my neck was so intoxicating. My wolf was going nuts, and I did not want to deny him.

Nyssa pulled away from me a bit, looking into my eyes. She pressed her soft red lips against mine. It felt so nice. I kissed her back with lust and passion. I took her to the room, laying her on the bed. She grabbed me, pulling me on top of her. She looked at me with shyness in her eyes. I started to kiss her more, running my hand down her body.

I could feel the heat coming from her body as we kissed. I felt her. She was calling to me as we kissed more and more. Nyssa rotated our bodies so I was now under her and she was on top of me. I looked up. Her eyes were no longer their normal color, but they were glowing yellow. I could see her wolf was coming out in the energy of the lust in us.

"Nyssa, do you accept me?" I asked her.

She looked at me. "Yes… I want you forever," she said, leaning in and kissing my neck. Nyssa ran her hands down the muscle of my stomach, coming to my pants. Before she could go any farther there was knocking coming from the front door.

92

I rolled her over on her back, getting up. I approached the door, picking up a scent, and I knew it could not be right. I opened the door to find Dante standing outside my door. He had on a pair of blue jeans, cowboy boots and a white sweater with a white jacket on.

"Long time no see, kiddo!" he said to me with a smile.

I was shocked to see him. "Dante! Is that really you?" I asked him.

He smiled at me "Yeah, lad, it's me. I made a vow to you and I intend to keep it. May I come in please?" he said walking passed me.

Nyssa came bouncing out of the room fixing her shirt. She stopped and looked at Dante, backing away from him slowly. "What are you doing here?" she asked him.

I looked at her and then looked at him. "What have I missed?" I said.

Nyssa walked passed Dante and stood behind me. "He is our leader. He is the prime," she said.

"What the hell do you mean our leader, and what is a prime?" I said.

Dante walked around looking at everything. "I am the Prime. I am the oldest living werewolf. So, since I am the eldest and one of the more powerful next to you, of course, chosen one. I was given the title of Prime by the council over five hundred years ago. So did Anoki show you the future?" he said picking up a picture of my family and me.

"Yes he did!" I replied walking over and taking the picture from him.

"Well let's not let that happen shall we. We need to find the weapon that can kill the vampire lord."

I set the picture down and turned to look at him. "What do you mean weapon?" I asked him.

93

Dante pulled out an old parchment from his pocket. He opened it setting it on the table. I looked down. It was a drawing of a knife. It looked to be very old in its design.

"What is this?"

Dante patted my back leaning in to look at the drawing. "This, my boy is the weapon that will end Vlad that vampire bastard."

I looked hard at the drawing trying to imagine this thing killing the vampire lord. "Well where is this bad boy blade at?" I asked Dante.

He picked the parchment up and put it back into his pocket. "That is the problem. Not even the council knows what happened to it. But I have an idea of someone who might know," he said with a smile.

Nyssa walked over touching my back. I looked over at her and I could see concern in her eyes. "No worries, love, we will be just fine. Besides I have killed a few vampires with Dante before. Isn't that right, old man?" I said with a chuckle.

Dante looked at Nyssa, and then back at me. "More like I killed some vampires and you took out one…"

I just shook my head. "We'll go. Nyssa, I want you to stay here. I just don't want you to get hurt, and once I reunite with Mira, she is going to want your blood." I could see tears forming in Nyssa eyes. I knew she wanted to help. But I could not let her get hurt because of the mistakes I made.

I followed Dante out of the house. We took his black SUV and headed through Canada. The drive was nice. I wanted to ask Dante about Olympia, but I did not want to stir up sadness in him. We did not head into the states; instead, we drove to Alberta. It was a small, cold place. I had never been there before. We stopped outside a baby blue colored house. It was located across the street from a strip club. Dante parked and we got out. Even though I was a werewolf I still could feel the cold winds on my warm skin.

"Who lives here?" I asked Dante.

94

His gaze passed over me. "This is where we will get the info on the weapon." I followed behind him taking in the darkness of the night.

Dante knocked on the white door. I could hear someone approaching the door. Then I felt Dante, he put his wolf to sleep. Then he looked at me and I did the same.

The door opened and a little old woman with short, curly, grey hair opened the door. "Yes, can I help you?" she said with a magical tone. I could feel it. She was no more human than I was.

"I am looking for Laura the blade maker," Dante said with a smile.

The little old woman looked at him, then at me. It was like she was trying to study us. "Why hide who you are, werewolf?" she said to Dante.

"I did not know how you felt about werewolves," Dante said with respect in his voice. The old women made a tisk, tisk sound and opened the door for us to enter.

We entered what looked like a regular home. There was nothing special about it at all. I turned and the old woman was gone. I looked over at Dante and he shrugged his shoulders. I followed Dante into another room where we found another female. She had red skin, black hair and long elfish ears. She wore a mechanics suit. As she looked at us she smiled. "So, I hear you are looking for me?"

Dante bowed before her. "Yes. I am Dante, Prime of the werewolf nation. I have come to seek your great wisdom. I am looking for the mythical blade that can kill the vampire lord."

Laura looked at Dante. She then turned and started to walk away. Dante and I followed her in another room, a stone room, as the previous room started to fade away. Heat blazed in the stone room. I stood with Dante in the room of a blacksmith.

"That blade does not exist…," she said to us.

95

Dante shook his head. I could see the anger in him. "What do you mean it does not exist?" Dante said with rage in his voice.

"It means that I have not crafted it yet. I made up the legend to keep the vampire lord from attacking my people. It was the greatest lie of the Iron forge elves. It kept him from invading our homelands."

Dante grabbed an unfinished knife throwing it across the room. "We need that weapon! We need to kill the vampire lord. If he lives the world will fall into darkness!"

"Even if I made the blade it would not matter. He would have to be killed by one of my kind or the chosen one," she said. Dante walked over and put his hand on my shoulder. "This is Liam Blackmane, werewolf born of the Tier bloodline. He is also the chosen one!"

Laura walked over to me touching my face with her red skinned hands. She looked at me with her glowing green eyes. I could feel her tapping into my inner wolf with her magic. He was stirring and becoming quite angry. She released me and stepped over to her forge. "It is true you are the prophesied chosen one. I never thought a werewolf would be the chosen one. I will make this blade for you. I need a few days. Once it is done I will find you."

Dante bowed before her once again. "Thank you, and I must say I rather enjoy your original form, that of the old woman."

Dante and I left the house and headed back to the states. "We need to stop and see a couple more people," he said with a smile. The drive took us a day and a half. We arrived in Avalon, Washington. It was a harbor town on the line between Canada and Washington. It was beautiful, the buildings that were from the early 1800's. The town was called the Gem of Washington, a place where dreams come true.

Chapter IX: Truths

As we pulled into Avalon, Dante drove us to a white three story Victorian house. It was stunning, the grass was emerald green. The house was surrounded by roses and many other beautiful flowers. "What are we doing here?" I asked him.

"You will see, now get out of the car," he said with a slight chuckle. I followed Dante into the house, where to my surprise I found Olympia alive and well. She looked the same as she had when I first met her, not aged a day.

"You survived, that is so great. I am happy you're alive," I said to her. She turned and smiled at me, but my face dropped when I saw her. She was with child, and I was not sure why they would chance it again.

"Do not worry, lad. This child is not going to come out like Kaliban."

I looked at him. "How do you know that?" I said with a growl.

Dante walked over to Olympia, placing his big hand on her very round stomach. "Because we have faith…" I laughed and then walked out the door of the house. "Where are you going, Liam?" Dante yelled to me from the front door.

I ignored him and kept walking down the street. I came upon a park where I decided to take a seat on one of the swings. I sat there, trying to get my head around why they would do something so stupid again. I was enjoying my peace and quiet then a gust of wind blew by me.

"Lost in thought?" a voice said to me.

I turned and found that I was no longer alone on the swings. I found Laura sitting by me. She looked like a little black-headed girl this time. I knew it was her because her scent did not change. "I have the weapon for you. Are you sure you are ready to do this? Killing the lord of all vampires is not something that is easy to do," she said handing me a black bladed knife with a white oak hilt.

97

I took the blade from her with my inner wolf, and I could feel the magic in it. "So how   does this work?" I asked her.

"You need to plunge that blade into his heart then into each of his eyes. The eyes are where the true soul lives. Good luck, and watch yourself around Dante. He is not to be trusted."

The same wind blew, and she was gone. Laura left me with the knife, and with new problems. I took the blade, hiding it underneath my jacket, and then decided to walk back to Dante's house. I stood outside the gate just looking up at the house. I was still very much angry with Dante and Olympia.

I knew it was none of my business, but I felt responsible for them. I looked around and saw the ones responsible for the beautiful yard and flowers. It was the gnomes; they kept it all tidy like Olympia wanted them to. I walked up opening the door. I found Dante and Olympia sitting in the parlor.

"Welcome back, Liam." Before I could say anything Olympia was up and running her hands in the air. It was like she was following something. "What is it my love?" Dante asked her. She walked over to me and opened my jacket. She backed up, away from the knife like she was afraid of it. "Is that the blade that will kill Vlad?" Dante asked me. I nodded. He got up and started to walk over to take the blade.

I closed my jacket and backed away from him. "What is the deal, Liam? Give it to me so I can keep it safe." As he said that, the words Laura said about him ran through my mind.

"NO! I think I will hold on to it. She told me to not let it out of my hands." What I told him was a lie, but I did not want him taking it.

"Okay, that is fine if that is what she said. Then that is how it must be."

I walked over and sat down on the love seat. "Dante, what happened to Kaliban?" I asked him.

98

Dante looked at Olympia and then back at me. "Kaliban escaped the night of the fire. I spent hundreds of years searching for him but I could not find him."

I looked at Dante and I could tell he was lying to me. "So what are we doing now? I got the weapon. Let's go kill this blood-sucking bastard!"

Dante shot up from the couch and looked at me. "We need to rest first then head into Seattle. I want to talk to the packs alpha there. See if they can help us take care of the vampire lord."

I felt that Dante was up to something, but I did not know what yet. But I would find out soon enough. Olympia got up and went into the kitchen, so I figured it was time for dinner.

Dante sat there looking at me I could see the anger in his eyes. He wanted this blade but I did not think it was to kill the vampire lord. "Did the blacksmith say anything more to you?" Dante asked me.

"Nope, not really… Just told me to keep it and how to kill the vampire lord. Why?" I asked him.

Dante stopped watching me and turned his attention to the photo above the fireplace. I looked over at the photo also; it was that of Olympia and the kids of the class she teaches at the elementary.

"Come on, boys, come eat!" Olympia yelled from the kitchen. I followed behind Dante into the dining room. He sat at the front of the table. I took a seat in the middle. The gnomes brought in the food using magic to make them float to the table. Olympia sat at the other end of the table. The gnomes where preparing her plate for her.

They served Olympia for she is their mother. We ate dinner in peace, no one said a word. It was one of my favorite meals. Pot roast and potatoes. I loved when my mother made it for me. When Dante was done he left his plate and walked up the stairs. The gnomes came by and cleaned up his mess like good little house slaves.

99

It was just Olympia and I in the dining room eating. I decided to take this time and get some answers. "How far along are you, Olympia?"

She took a small bite of the potatoes before looking up at me. "I am 8 months. Soon she will be born, and we will be able to save Kaliban," she replied.

I looked at her not sure what she meant by that. "It's a girl, huh? That is good. Can I ask you, how is she going to save Kaliban?"

Olympia looked at me, and then just got up and left the room. I sat there trying to figure out what was going on. I decided that it was better for me to go and do this on my own. I left the house walking down the street heading into downtown.

The sun was setting and I needed to find a place to sleep for the night. I came across a hotel called Excalibur Inn, it was a hotel shaped like a castle. I got a room and decided to call it a night. As I opened the door to my room I felt like I was at some dumb amusement park. I took my coat off tossing it on the chair. The knife I placed underneath the mattress.

The bed was nice, it was comfortable but I laid there thinking about Nyssa. Then I heard a voice. "Liam! Why have you abandoned me?" The voice kept repeating it over and over. Then it clicked, it was Mira. We still had the bond. I tried to picture only Nyssa hoping to block Mira out of my mind. I rolled over facing the door. I closed my eyes and soon found myself asleep. I started to dream. I was in my old bedroom. I looked over and saw Mira in all white, sitting on my bed. She smiled at me. "Am I dreaming?" I asked her.

She stood up walking over to me, placing her right hand on my chest. "Liam, I miss you, my love… why have you abandoned me for another?" she said to me.

"Mira, I am sorry but you and I can never be together. I have found someone who makes me happy and I love her. Besides, I will come for your father and I will kill him," I replied to her.

100

Mira turned walking over to the window and looking out it. "You know, Liam, you and I are still bonded. You can never leave me. I will not allow it."

I started to walk towards her but she vanished like smoke. I looked around, and the room started to fade also. I soon found myself standing naked in the middle of a green field. The sky was clear with white clouds. The sun was high and felt warm on my skin. Now this was a dream I liked to have.

"It's beautiful here, is it not?" I turned and found the Great Spirit standing behind me.

"Why have you invaded my dream?" I asked her.

She smiled at me. "You are one of my great children I wanted to make sure you are ok. Besides I needed to save you from the child demon."

I hated that my dreams where open for anyone to join. I quickly tried to cover up my goods. The Great Spirit saw me and waved her hand to me. A black roman type of robes appeared covering me up. "I can see that you did not listen to me. I told you not to bond with that vampire. Look at you now, stuck with her for all time."

I dropped my head. I knew she was right. I was ashamed at myself.

The Great Spirit touched my chin, bringing my eyes up. I looked at her and I could see only concern and love. "I can help you escape the bond," she said with a smile.

I could tell by her eyes she was telling the truth. "How can you break the bond?" I asked her with excitement in my voice. She let go of my face and walked away from me. I watched her as she started to move her hand through the empty air. Soon the clouds of my dream started to come together forming the shape of a mirror. I started to walk forward as she touched the newly formed mirror. It rippled like a stone dropping in a pond.

The mirror started to brighten up like a light shooting out of it. I covered my eyes keeping the light from hitting them. As the light

101

faded I removed my arm to see Mira standing over her father's dead body. "The blade that the blacksmith gave you can also free you. You must take Mira's life after you kill her father. His blood must enter into her. The power will overwhelm her own. Before she dies you must drink of her taking in her and her father's blood. This will break the bond between master and slave. This will free you from losing your brother wolf in the act of killing her." I felt a release of freedom come over me. I was finally going to be free of that liar and live my life with Nyssa.

The Great Spirit blew into the mirror making it fade away. Then she walked over kissing me in the middle my forehead. "It is time for you to wake up, a new day awaits you."

I awoke to the sound of a car pulling up to the hotel. The sun was up and I felt as if I had not slept that night. I got up, still in the clothes from the prior day. I soon picked up the scent of Dante. "Come in." The door opened and Dante stood there. He walked in closing the door behind him. "Why did you leave?" he said sitting in a chair.

I looked at him and all that I could think of is what the blacksmith said to me. "I really do not know," I told him. "I was still a bit angry that you and your mate are having another baby. I know it's none of my business but something about it is weighing on me."

Dante started to laugh. "Do not worry, boy. I know it's something that we should have thought about more. But I believe that this new child will not be like Kaliban. Olympia talked to the fairy sprits. They told her this child would free us all." Dante got up holding his hand out to me. I looked at him not sure if I should take it or not. I grabbed his hand. He pulled me up from the bed, patting my back. "Come on, chosen one. We have much work to do," he said as we exited the hotel room.

I got into his black SUV. I was not sure what was ahead of us. But I knew I had to ride the train with Dante until it was time. We left Avalon and headed down the highway driving through the great forest of Washington. It was a relaxing drive, the forest called to me and my wolf. I wanted to forget all my problems and

102

just get lost in the forest forever. We drove into another small town to fuel up. It was a logging community, you could tell by all the logging trucks in the town. The smell of ash and cedar flowed through the air. After fueling up we left the town and headed to Seattle. Dante still had plans on meeting up with the Seattle alpha. He did not tell me what he had planned. I was in the dark.

We finally made it into Seattle, the sea carrying itself through the currents of the air. We arrived at a warehouse down at the docks. It had a giant 29 painted on the side of it. Outside the doors were two wolves in human form. Dante and I exited the car. As soon as they saw Dante they dropped their gazes. "Move!" Dante said pushing the doors open. We entered into the warehouse. I walked closely behind Dante. My wolf was going nuts, he wanted to kill everyone. I did not know why he was being like this.

"Dante… Welcome to my home."

I looked over and saw a man that stood about 6 ft. tall. He had on a pair of black slacks with a white button down shirt. His skin had the color of someone from the Middle East. His black hair was kept short and trimmed.

I looked around; the warehouse looked like a house and bar built into one. "Is there somewhere private we can talk, Giovanni?" The alpha looked around and his pack started to leave us. Soon it was just us alone with the alpha.

"So what brings you to my door?" Giovanni asked Dante.

Dante looked around making sure everyone was gone. "I need you and your pack to help us kill Vlad."

Giovanni stepped back. I could smell the fear he had.

He looked over at me, " Why would you want to kill the vampire lord? Are you not the wolfguard to the princess?" he asked me.

I felt as if he was talking down to me and I hated it. "I have come to see that I was lied to by the vampires. Everything I felt was a lie. I made a terrible mistake believing them. Mira wanted

103

me only for a slave," I replied back with a growl in my harsh voice.

I watched him as he winced at my voice. I knew my power had made an impression on him. Dante looked back at me with a frown on his face. I just smiled back at him. I enjoyed making the alpha squirm with my power.

Giovanni turned his eyes from me and onto Dante. "So what is the plan?" he said with obedience.

"Show him the blade, Liam." I opened up my coat and pulled the blade from my side. I held it out to let Giovanni see it. "This blade is the only weapon that can kill Vlad the vampire lord. With this, we will free ourselves from the slavery they offer us as wolfguards. With Liam, we have the chosen one on our side, we cannot fail."

I could still see the doubt in Giovanni's eyes, and he did not want anything to do with this. But because Dante was proclaimed king of the werewolves, he had no choice but to obey. "When do you want my pack?" he asked Dante.

Dante looked over at me and then back at Giovanni. "By next week! We are going to kill that blood sucking demon and his entire coven." I was lost. Dante did not inform me of any of this. I hated that he was keeping me in the dark.

"We will be ready. Do you want me to reach out to other packs?" he asked.

"Yes, make sure you tell them that I am not asking but telling!"

The power of his voice hit Giovanni like a Mack truck. But it was weird, I could feel the power but it did not faze me one bit. I turned and walked out leaving Dante alone in the warehouse. I walked down the docks taking in the sight of the ocean.

"Excuse me?" I turned and saw a young boy. He was at least fifteen, very young to be a werewolf. He had on a blue zip up sweater, jeans and a pair of red converse shoes.

104

"Yes?" I replied to him.

"Is it true that you are the chosen one?" he asked with a small voice. I could feel the fear on him, he was scared of me.

"Yes it is true. I am Liam Blackmane, proclaimed chosen one," I said to him with a bit of a smartass remark. I had seen a smile start to peek out of his face. I wanted to make him not fear me.

"I am Jason Ryder. I just became a werewolf a month ago. I killed my family and Giovanni found me hiding down here. He took me in and has been teaching me to control my werewolf urges."

I walked over to the boy placing my hand on his shoulder and looking him in the eye. "Being one of the children of the moon is a gift. Remember that with this great power comes a responsibility to keep it under control. In time you will learn to become one with your wolf, bonding in a brotherhood with him. Listen to your wolf, he will always watch out for you." I let go of him and started to walk more down the pier. I watched the ocean crash on the shore on the beach by the docks. I loved the smell of the ocean air; it was intoxicating like a beautiful painting or image. I came up to a man sitting on the side of the dock fishing. He had on a yellow slicker, jacket and pants. His feet dangled over the edge of the dock.

"Are you going to stand there or come over and join me?" he said not taking his eyes away from the sea.

I walked over taking a seat next to him. He handed me one of the three fishing poles he had in the water. "Keep the line steady and do not let it go."

I grabbed ahold of the pole and I could feel the line tugging. Whatever was on it was strong; I had to call upon my wolf to keep the pole from leaving my hands. It took a bit to get the pole under control.

"So tell me, wolf, what is on your mind?" the fishermen said to me.

105

I wanted to look at him but I could not take my eyes off the line. "I feel like I have the entire world sitting on my shoulders. I know that I am no longer human. But I am still so young and I do not know if I am ready for this," I said tugging on the line a bit.

I managed to take a quick look over at the fishermen and he held his pole steady one handed. In his other hand he had a beer. "Sometimes life is given a push in the direction that we need to follow. You might be young, but you truly are the one chosen to take on this train you call a ride. Remember that everything happens for a reason." A wave splashed up onto the docks knocking me over. I lost the fishing pole and the strange fisherman was gone. I got up looking out into the ocean. Then I saw the fishermen, he was walking on top the water. I started to walk back to the warehouse. I found Dante talking with one of the pack wolves outside. He was propped up against his SUV.

"Let's get out of here and go get some dinner," I said to Dante, getting into the SUV. He patted the wolf's shoulder and climbed in after me. I looked over at Dante as he started to drive the SUV. "Dante, tell me…Why do you hate the vampire lord so bad?" I asked him.

He did not respond quickly. A few moments passed before he said anything. "Remember the fire that almost took Olympia from me. Well, it was the vampire lord and his lackeys that started it. He also has Kaliban, and has been using him like a dog." I could hear the pain in his voice. I now understood why he wanted the vampire lord dead.

106

Chapter X: Friendships are Tested

Dante and I stayed the night at the local Motel 9. It was owned by the Seattle pack. I woke up to find Dante gone, and so was the blade. I had hid it underneath my mattress. I have no idea how he got it. I got up, grabbed some clothes from my pack and got dressed. I needed to find Dante before something bad happened. I headed outside taking in a long sniff of the air. I needed to pick up his scent. I caught just enough of his scent to point me in a direction. I followed it until I came to a small coin shop.

It looked to be closed but I could hear someone moving inside. I grabbed the door handle ripping the door from the hinges. I walked in looking around. It smelled of musk and dust. "Whoever you are, I know you are here!" I yelled through the store. I stood looking around waiting for whoever it was decided to come out.

"Look, I am not here for you. I am just looking for something that was stolen from me," I said as I walked down the narrow aisle. I heard a door in the back open; I stood waiting for whomever it was to emerge. Soon a man in his forties walked out from the back. He had on a stained white shirt with khaki pants and flip-flops. He had pale skin with brown curly hair.

"Please, do not hurt me!" he said with his hands up.

"I know Dante came this way. I am just looking for him. Tell me where he went, and I won't hurt you," I said to him with anger in my voice.

He lowered his hands still looking at me. His fear was all over the room; it was as if it was flowing out of him. "I can't tell you. If I do, he will kill me!"

I walked closer to him, my eyes glowing yellow. My wolf was coming to the surface I could feel him. "If you do not tell me, I will kill you!" I said to him with an evil smile.

"Okay, okay, I will tell you. He is heading to the docks to catch a boat. That is all I know - I swear to you." I could see the truth in his eyes. I knew he was telling me the truth and only the truth. I turned around and left the coin shop. I caught a taxi and arrived at the docks.

As I got out, I saw Dante; he was just getting onto a small boat. "DANTE!!!" I yelled to him. He turned to me and quickly had the captain take the boat out to sea.

I ran down to the entrance of the port he left from. I watched him sail away with the only blade that could kill Vlad. "FUCK!!" I yelled in to the heavens.

"What is wrong?" I turned to find the fishermen standing behind me. He stood there smiling at me.

"That bastard stole something important from me," I said to him.

He walked around me, looking at the boat sailing away. "I might be able to help you," he said with a smile. I looked over at him; he was stroking his long grey beard.

"And what would you want in return?" I asked him.

He walked over to the edge of the dock and spit into the water. I watched as the water started to glow, then become clear as day. I could see his trail. "One day I will come to you needing a favor. But until then I am going to give you what you want," he said. He turned around and touched my forehead with his finger. I felt a surge of energy flow into me from him.

"What the hell was that?" I asked him.

He looked at me and then shoved me into the water. But instead of sinking, I was standing on the water. "Through me you can follow the trail. Good luck, and I will see you soon, Liam Blackmane." I watched as he turned into a puddle flowing into the ocean.

I started to follow the trail he set for me. I was nervous because I could see all the fish swimming underneath me. After an hour of following the trail, I came to a small personal dock. The boat was docked, and I headed out of the water and started to follow the

108

wooden path. I decided in case I found him, I should hide my werewolf side. Just like he showed me, I made my wolf go to sleep. Now if he picked up my scent I would smell like a regular human. I soon came up to a lake house and I could see Dante. He was talking to a blonde female inside the house. I walked slowly up to the porch outside the house. I let my rage flow, and my wolf awoke. Dante turned and saw me. It took me less than a second to break the sliding glass and grab Dante.

I lifted him from the ground, letting his feet dangle. It was weird that he did not even try to break free from my grip. "Tell me why… Why did you steal the knife and run from me?"

Dante looked at me. His blue eyes had fear in them. "I am sorry, Liam, but plans change and I cannot kill Vlad any longer. He promised me if I brought him the knife, he would free Kaliban. I am sorry, but my son is more important to me. I had to do as he told me to."

I flung Dante against the wall. "Please do not destroy my house," the blonde said to me. I turned and just glared at her, and she quickly looked away. Dante picked himself up from the ground. I expected him to try and attack me, but he just stood there not making a move.

"Where is the blade?" I asked Dante.

He looked over at the blonde girl. I looked over at her also, and she walked over to the cabinet in the living room. She pulled out the blade and set it on the counter. "Take it and get the hell out of my house, you fucking dog!" she said crying.

"Liam, please do not do this. When we get Kaliban back, we can find another way to kill him. I swear to you, on my honor."

I grabbed the blade and looked at him. "You are pathetic. How the hell can you be the proclaimed werewolf king? And do not speak about honor. You do not know the meaning of honor. If I see you again, I will kill you, so make sure you stay away from me."

I went out the broken sliding door and then headed back down to the docks. I found that the trail was still glowing, so I guessed I could still follow it. I stepped slowly onto the water and did not sink. I decided to run back to the docks instead of walking. I arrived in five minutes instead of an hour. As soon as I was about to jump up to the dock I felt the energy slip away. I fell into the ocean. I swam to shore trying to shake off some of the water.

I found Giovanni looking at me. He had on just a pair of board shorts. I take it he was basking in some sun. "What are you doing Liam?" he asked me.

I looked back at the ocean and then at him. "Let's just say that we need to have a long talk," I said to him. He nodded and I followed him back to the warehouse. Giovanni gave me some dry clothes and left me alone to change. The clothes fit pretty well. I headed out of the room and into the main room.

Giovanni had on a plain white t-shirt and was pouring us two beers. "So, what is it we need to talk about?" he asked me handing me a beer.

I know I was not twenty-one, but I know I will never age so it doesn't matter.

"Dante is no longer our king. He will not be coming with us when we take on the vampire lord. I also want to tell you that if you and your pack do not want to come, that is okay," I said to him.

He set his beer down on the table and just looked at me. "Wait, what do you mean Dante is no longer our Prime? How could that have happened?" he asked me.

"I am your chosen one and Dante tried to stab us in the back. He took the blade and was going to give it to the vampire lord. He cannot be trusted, not now, and not ever. Look, I know I am just a young wolf but I also know that I have to watch out for all of you. I do not know why, but my wolf tells me it is our job."

Giovanni grabbed his beer. "Well, lad, I offer you my loyalty and oath that my pack and I will be there for you." Giovanni and I tapped our beers and drank to his oath. We finished our beers and Giovanni looked to his front door. It opened and his second,

110

Luther, walked in. He was a tall black man wearing a green and yellow shirt. His shorts and flip-flops were also green and yellow.

"Hey, boss man, who is the kid?" he asked walking over to the bar.

"This kid is our savior, he is the chosen one destined to end the vampire lords life."

Luther grabbed his martini and walked over sitting on the black love seat. "That is epic. Sorry, kid, that is one hard line to follow. So what does this have to do with us?" he asked Giovanni.

"It is funny you mentioned that, my friend. We are going to help him kill the vampire bastard," he replied with a smile.

Luther took a sip of his drink and smiled back at Giovanni. I was going to spend the rest of the day hanging with Giovanni and his pack. But plans change. The warehouse doors opened and in walked the winged crusader Teagan. He had a black suit on and was looking like a lawyer. "Liam, we need to go," he said looking around.

Luther looked at Teagan and then to me. "Looks like you might get touched by an angel," he said laughing.

"Real funny… Why do we need to leave?" I asked Teagan.

"Because it is almost game day and, well, the vampires are looking for you. Besides I got one more lesson I want you to learn," he said to me.

I was not sure why but I felt uneasy about Teagan coming. I would have felt better if it was Anoki, but with Teagan… something was off about him.

"Where is Anoki?" I asked Teagan.

He stopped looking around and started staring at me. "I am not going to sit here and debate this with you, Liam. I need you to come with me. It is for your own protection, as for Anoki, well, he is a bit tied up right now," he said with a smile on his face.

111

"I do not think I will be going anywhere with you," I said.

Giovanni and Luther stood up blocking Teagan from me. They stood their ground like guards.

"I do not understand why you are being like this. I am on your side," he said.

"Let's just say that nothing is adding up. And you showed up out of the blue, that is a little weird. I am thinking I will be safer here with Giovanni and Luther. So, thanks, but no thanks."

Teagan shook his head and in a flash of white light he was gone. Giovanni and Luther stood down taking their seats again.

"Man, what was up with that dude?" Luther said finishing his drink.

I looked at them both. "I don't know, maybe I am just being paranoid," I said.

Giovanni set his beer down and looked at me. "No… you were not. I could smell something evil about him. He was no longer the heavenly angel. He was here to collect you and us being here was not something he expected."

"Thank you guys for what you did," I said to them.

Luther just nodded his head and Giovanni smiled. "It is no problem. You are our savior, so that is what we had to do. Besides, I was not about to let you be taken from my territory against your will. I think you should crash here tonight, the spare room is in the back," he said getting up.

He left the room and went into his room. Luther left the warehouse locking the doors. I found the spare room, and it was a lavish place. It put some of the hotels I stayed at to shame. I laid down on the bed and just felt complete comfort, it was amazing.

I found myself dozing off almost instantly. I slept better than I had before. I awoke to the smell of steak and eggs being made. I stepped out of the room to find a young girl who could not be more

112

than thirteen. She had on a long brown skirt, a brown top and her strawberry colored hair was in a ponytail.

She turned and looked at me. "Morning sunshine. Are you hungry?" she said with a smile.

"Who might you be?" I asked her.

She was about to tell me when Giovanni answered. "She is Jenifer, my daughter, who should be at her mother's house. Isn't that right, girl?" he said with a smile.

She grabbed two plates and set them at the table. Then she walked about to her father, kissing his cheek. "Sure whatever you say, daddy. I got to go, school starts in thirty minutes."

Giovanni patted her head and she skipped out of the warehouse. "Well, let's eat, I guess. Sorry about that, it's usually her mom's turn to keep her. Sometimes I think that girl has too much of me in her," he said with a chuckle. I was still trying to figure out how she was his daughter since she did not look anything like him.

"Why does she look, well, not like you?" I asked him.

He just took a bite of his steak and smiled. "It is one of those genetic things; she came out white with red hair like her Irish mother. I love that girl."

We finished our breakfast and I found my clothes washed and folded on the chair. "And who do I have to thank for this?" I said to Giovanni.

"I am thinking my little hell raiser. She probably found them and decided to wash them for you," he said putting our dishes in the sink.

I got up grabbed my clothes and hit the shower in the guest room. When I came out I found Giovanni on his laptop talking to someone. "Giovanni! Can you tell me where I can find the altar of Anoki?" I asked him.

He looked over at me. "That would be on the eastside of Seattle, in Green Harper Park," he said to me.

113

I looked at him, he tossed me a wave and I left. I needed to find Anoki, so I got a taxi and headed to the park. As soon as we pulled up I could see how it got the name. The park was a beautiful color of green; it was almost unnatural how green it was. I walked through the park looking for the altar. I soon found it. "Alright Anoki, I need your guidance. Where are you?" I said trying to pray. Nothing happened so I figured he was really busy. I turned to walk away when I heard something.

"Liam… can you hear me?"

I swore it was Anoki, but I could not see him. "Anoki is that you?" I said to the altar.

"Listen closely, Liam… Teagan betrayed us. He has betrayed the council and joined sides with Vlad. He captured me and imprisoned me in a giant oak tree here in the park. You can free me. I need you to get salt and make a circle around it. Then you will have to chant these words - Desmones, Triconian, and Empersian. Once you say these words my bonds will break, and I can do the rest. Now get going, and please hurry."

I turned and left the altar, heading to a store I saw on my way. I paid for a box of salt and made my way back to the park. It took me a few minutes to find the giant oak. It was hidden deep into the park and had a strange red aura around it.

I poured the circle of salt and chanted the words. I stepped back and the ground started to shake like an earthquake. I watched as the tree exploded sending splinters of wood flying. A red glowing being stood where the tree was. "Anoki?" I said. The red glow faded and Anoki dropped to the ground.

He was steaming. "Good job, kid. Good job. Now let's get out of here." Anoki grabbed me and wisped me with him. But this time instead of landing on my feet, I came flying out of the portal slamming into a tree.

"Damn it, Anoki!" I said, rubbing my head.

Anoki stood over me, helping me up. "Sorry about that, Liam, I am still a bit weak so it was a rough ride. But, hey, we made it to

114

my home." I looked around and saw that is was an open field with giant trees surrounding it.

I saw little wooden trees moving around. "What are those?" I asked Anoki.

He looked over at the wooden fairies. "Oh, those are my creation. I made them to keep the forest well kept. I call them Mojo's wood fairies. Now come on, let's go inside."

I was thinking, what he is talking about? This is just a field, but I turned my head and found a hill with a wooden door. Anoki opened it with his big red hands. "Well, wolf, are you coming in?" he asked smiling.

I followed him inside. I had to rub my eyes because what I was seeing was unbelievable. Every room was made of wood, beautifully carved wood. I followed behind Anoki until we reached a room with a giant throne in it.

Anoki took his seat and started to glow. "You were never meant to see this place. This is my personal realm, not even Teagan can come here," he said to me.

"Anoki, why are you glowing?" I asked him.

He just smiled at me. "We, the great spirits of power, come back to our personal realms to recharge. Me, being here in this throne is like a charger for me. Besides, I am not the energizer bunny, I don't keep going and going," he said with a loud laugh.

He soon closed his eyes and fell asleep. I decided to snoop around while he took his energy sleep. I walked into the last room and watched the wall. That is right, watched it. The paintings all moved like a picture show. It showed the outside world but in paintings, it was actually very unreal. I reached up touching one of the pictures and it started to glow, then took up the whole wall. The painting stopped being a painting and looked to be clear like a television. I could see people walking around the park where Anoki was imprisoned.

The place where the tree was now had a fountain in its place. It was weird. I touched the picture again and it shrunk back to a painting. The other paintings appeared again. I looked around and found a painting that was very interesting to me. It was of Nyssa, she was outside picking flowers. I touched the painting and turned it into a wall television. "I miss you so much, Nyssa." I said.

Then something weird happened, Nyssa started to look around. "Liam is that you?" she said.

What the, can she hear me? "Nyssa, can you hear me?" I said to her.

She looked around searching for me. "Yes, dummy, I can hear you, now where the hell are you at?" she said with a demanding tone.

"Well, I am in the realm of Anoki; he brought me here because Teagan has betrayed the council," I replied to her demand.

"Wow, really? What is it like there? Oh, and Teagan, yeah, well, he came by here looking for you a few days ago."

I started to become angry. I hated that he came to her.

"Teagan went there? I need you to stay away from him. I got to go, honey. I hear Anoki. He is waking up. I will be home soon." I touched the picture, and it shrank back into a painting.

I walked back into the throne room, and Anoki was opening his eyes. "God, that felt good. What were you doing while I slept?" he said.

"Well, I found your picture room. It was amazing."

He laughed at me. "I made that room over five hundred years ago. I got bored. Every place I visit a new painting appears. This is how I see so much. I have used it to keep an eye on you for a long time. I know, peeping tom, right? But I promise I do not watch the juicy parts."

I shook my head not sure how to reply to that. Anoki got up from his throne and headed to the picture room. I followed behind

116

him. He stopped and then touched a painting, it grew larger. It was the vampire lord's mansion. "Watch," he said to me. He double clicked the painting with his finger and soon we were inside the house. The vampire lord and Teagan were sitting on the couches talking. I also saw Hannibal, and to my surprise, Dante.

"Even now the traitors are plotting a way to find you and end your life. This is why I took you from the mortal realm."

I watched as Teagan looked up as if he could see us. Then he flicked his fingers and the picture soon became only static.

"Damn, he just destroyed my little peek-a-boo hole. Oh, well, we know what they want and what they are doing." Anoki turned and we left that room to enter a new one. It was a dining room, and on the table was every kind of food you could think of.

Anoki took a seat, so I did as well. The food just seemed to appear, whatever kind I was thinking. I soon found a pepperoni pizza on my plate. I took a bite and sure enough it was from my favorite pizzeria, Tony's Pizza House. It had been so long since I had tasted something this good. I looked over and Anoki had a weird red fruit on his plate. "What is that you are eating?" I asked Anoki. He tore a piece from his fruit and tossed it to me.

It landed on top of my pizza. "Take a bite and tell me what you taste," he said with a giant smile.

I took the fork from the table and pulled a piece of the fruit off. I placed it in my mouth and it tasted like a strawberry, but it was not a strawberry.

"Why does it taste like a strawberry?" I asked Anoki.

"I created this fruit. I call it the memory fruit. It tastes like the fruit that you love the most. Is it not amazing or what?" he said poking it.

I finished the fruit and then started to work on my pizza. Before I could finish my meal the room started to shake. "Um… Anoki what is that?" I said looking around.

117

He stood up and went to the picture room. He touched a picture and it showed the outside. It was Teagan and he was firing some kind of energy at the door. "I thought you said he could not come to your realm?"

Anoki looked at me and laughed. "Well, damn, I guess I was wrong. Oh, well, let's go to the back room and take the back door out."

I followed Anoki to the throne room. He pushed on the wall in the back and it opened. He grabbed me tossing me through. "Go to your home, there you will be safe for your great mother watches over you," he said as he closed the door. I turned to find myself in the woods behind my home in Wasilla.

Chapter XI: Nightmares & Dreams

I ran as hard and as fast as I could. I wanted nothing more than to take Nyssa into my arms and never let her go. I saw the house. It started to become clearer as I got near it. But something in my heart and gut felt wrong. I slowed down to a jog looking around and smelling the air. I was looking for scents that should not be there. I soon picked up a scent that definitely should not be there. It was Mira. She was near but I could not see her. I walked up to the house and my heart stopped when I saw Mira. She was inside the house walking around. I soon feared for Nyssa. I rushed into the house breaking the door to get inside.

Mira turned and looked at me, a smile growing on her face. "So melodramatic aren't we, Liam?" she said as she sat on the couch.

"Where is she, TELL ME!!" I yelled.

Mira just looked at me blankly with no emotion on her face. "She is fine for now, but you and I need to talk. You have broken your vow to me. You are to be my guardian, my personal protector. Liam, I know we have not seen eye to eye, but I will let you come back. I will forgive all that has happened and let you stand at my side once again as my wolfguard. If you do this, I will release Nyssa. Oh, and you must hand over the blade. This is non-negotiable, as per my father."

I looked at Mira, and rage filled me. All I wanted was to shift and rip out her throat. "I will never become your slave again. The bond between us will soon be gone. I will not rest until I am free of you and your blood-sucking race. I will kill your father and then you. I swear to the gods you will all be dead. Now, I am going to give you a chance to give me back Nyssa and survive this night," I said to her with a growl.

She laughed at me and stood up from the couch. "Silly little wolf, I am not here to negotiate with you. I came to offer you a chance to save the ones you love and live a long and healthy life. Besides, Nyssa is not the only one I have that you care about." Mira pulled out a chain with my pendant on it. "Look, your sister is here with us also!" she said laughing.

119

I stood helpless, unable to stop her from taking Nyssa and my sister. Mira walked out the door. I followed her out not sure what I was going to do. I found my path blocked by two vampires in black suits. I took them to be her bodyguards. "Mira, please do not do this!" I yelled to her.

She turned and just smiled at me. "Sorry, Liam, the choice was yours. So now you have to live with the consequence of your actions. I will always love you, my wolfguard," she said before vanishing.

I started to growl at the two vampires who did not leave as she did. "If I were you, I would follow your master before I make you my dinner for tonight." The vampires looked at each other and then turned to look at me. One of the vampires grabbed me, holding me tight in a bear hug. His strength was unreal. I found it a bit hard to break free. I broke his hold, rolling across the grass away from them. I stood up and started to push the change. I needed to be in my wolf form to take them. The vampires started to charge me, but then something unexpected happened. Two lightning bolts shot out of the clear blue sky. Each of the bolts hit one of the vampires, disintegrating them instantly.

I stopped the changing reverting back to my human form. I looked around seeing no dark cloud in the sky. "That will teach those abominations from messing with one of my wolves," a voice echoed from the sky. I soon realized it was the Great Spirit who killed them.

"I could have taken them," I said to the sky.

"I am sure you could have but I beat you to it," she said to me.

"Great Spirit, why do you watch over me but let the blood princess take Nyssa? She is also one of your great children of the moon." The voice went silent for a moment.

"Sometimes things have to play out like the fates set it up to be. Nyssa has a role to play in the coming war, but you are the chosen one. I must protect you at all costs, and if I let anything happen to you, Anoki would not be pleased. He has been waiting for you for a very long time. I must go, but I need you to travel to Winter Horn Harbor, Maine. There you will find what you are looking for."

Before I could respond the Great Spirit was gone. I really hated how these all-powerful spirits of the earth act. So cryptic when it comes to the most simple of things.

I took Nyssa's truck to Anchorage, Alaska to catch a plane to Maine. It was going to be a very long flight. It took less than an hour to get to Anchorage. I got on flight 341 nonstop to Rockland, Maine. Like I predicted, it was a terribly long and boring flight.

After touching down in Rockland, I rented a car and headed north to Winter Horn Harbor. It took me over two hours and then a ferry ride. Winter Horn Harbor is an isolated island off the coast of Maine. I drove off the ferry and headed into the island town.

The town was quiet and very beautiful. The land was covered in green grass and flowers. It was almost as if it was too good to be true. I stopped at a small diner called Ray's place. It was decorated in the fifties era. I enjoyed it. The waitress was an older woman. She sat me at the booth in the corner. I had many eyes on me and I knew I was like the new shinny toy in town. She handed me a menu and trotted off. I looked at the menu trying to decide what was going to be for lunch.

"First time on the island?" I dropped the menu to find an older Native American man. He had tan skin and long salt and pepper hair. He had beads and feathers twisted into his hair. By the scent of the man he was not human, he smelled of magic.

"Yes it is, and you might be?" I asked him.

"Um, you okay, son?" the waitress asked me.

I looked at her not sure what she meant. "Yeah, of course, can I get a burger and fries with a chocolate shake please? And whatever the old man wants," I said to her.

She looked at me with her hands on her hips. "What are you talking about? You are alone in this booth, kiddo!" she said with a smile.

I turned my eyes from her and back onto the old Native American man. He just sat there, smiling. "Sorry boy she cannot see me, only you can. Now let's get down to business, shall we? What brings a werewolf to our small town?" he asked me.

I hated being so dense when it comes to the supernatural community. I had no idea how he knew who I was. "I was sent here by the Great Spirit. She told me I would find what I was looking for. I just have no idea what I am looking for," I said to him.

I looked up then and saw the waitress looking at me. I could tell by her look, she thought I was Grade A nuts. She placed my plate down, left the check and left me alone.

"So you came here because you were told to, but you have no idea what you are looking for? I would say that you are definitely lost then."

I took a bite of my burger and a sip of my shake. "Who are you and what are you?" I asked him while I continued to eat.

He reached over taking a fry and tossing it in his mouth. "I am no one and then I am someone. They call me Nashani, the guide of lost souls. As for what I am, well, that is something we can talk about some other time. Right now, let's just focus on you and let's see if we can find you some answers," he said eating another fry.

I looked down and noticed my plate was clean. This thing ate my food.

"Let's go, I got something to show you," the old Native American said getting out of the booth. I left the bill and money on the table.

I walked outside and the old man was heading down towards the harbor. I followed him leaving the rental car parked outside the diner. I watched as Nashani walked onto the beach, letting his bare feet digging into the sand.

"Why are we here?" I said to him.

He turned and looked. "They call this beach the Heartless Shore. Some say if you close your eyes, you can hear what your soul wants you to hear."

I looked out into the deep blue sea and closed my eyes. I tried to block everything out except for the beating of my heart. I found my subconscious taking over. I was no longer on the beach but standing outside a volcano. I know weird, right? I started to look around. I found that there was no heat.

Instead it felt icy cold; it gave me goose bumps on my arms. "Hello there, Liam." I turned and found myself standing on top a giant plateau. Standing in front of me was the old fisherman. But he no longer had on the yellow slicker and pants. Instead he had on a blue jogging suit with blue Nikes. His sea green hair was in a tight braid that ran down his back. "I did not expect to see you so soon," he said to me.

I walked to the edge of the plateau and looked down. There was a massive red river running below it. "Where are we?" I asked him.

He walked over and stood next to me. "This, my friend, is your mind, not mine. I do not even know how you pulled me in to it."

I stepped away from the edge. "Me either, by the way, who are you?" I asked him.

He smiled and laughed. "I was wondering how long until you would ask me that. Let me introduce myself. I am Triton, son of the great god of the sea, Poseidon."

I looked at him lost in what he said. So I guess every tale of every mythological thing is real. "Why have you been helping me?" I asked him.

"Let's just say that I was given the order to help you whenever I could. Some of the major players in the supernatural world want you to win. One of them is my father. He told me he owed your creator a favor," he replied.

I looked into the sky and it started to cloud over with thick, dark thunderclouds. "Do you have any ideas on why I created a place

123

like this and summoned you to it?" I asked. The clouds above started to let a tidal wave of rain pour down on us. The world I created started to run like it was a painting.

"Hey, Liam, can you maybe try and picture a new place for us to go to?" I closed my eyes picturing the only thing I could, the beach I was on. I felt a pull on me and then I was spinning through a tunnel made of bright colors. I could not see Triton anymore, he was not with me. I felt like Alice did when she fell down the rabbit hole.

The tunnel disappeared and I found myself laying on the beach face first. I sat up spitting sand out of my mouth and my clothes were soaked. I looked around and I was alone. The beach was foggy and cold. "HELLO!" I yelled. But, like I expected, no one answered. I started to walk down the beach looking for anyone who could help. The beach seemed to never end. I felt like I was going in circles. "NASHANI!" I yelled, but like my other pleas for help there was no answer. Then I saw a light off in the distance. I followed it until I came to a lighthouse. Then something weird happened, my body started to shift and I was not calling upon my wolf. My clothes started to tear, my bones were breaking. I had not felt this much pain shifting in a very long time. It was like the very first time happening all over again.

The shift was done, and I stood there feeling the warm and wet sand on my newly created paws. I took in a deep breath, not picking up anything in the air. No scents, nothing. "Well, you are a pretty white wolf aren't you." I turned my head and saw Nashani, who just looked at me. "How do I get out of this hell of a dream?" I asked him.

To my surprise, he could understand me. "Like I told you before, that is up to you. This dream walk is the way to answers," he said to me. "Damn it, Wolf, how did you pull me into this one with you again?"

Nashani and I turned to see Triton standing behind us. "Please tell me you did not summon this pagan to come help you," Nashani said to me. I looked at them both. I could sense hatred passing between them. My attention from them was soon adverted when

124

the sky set ablaze. Nashani and Triton looked up at the sky as a giant black figure fell. It hit the ocean causing a massive cloud of steam to engulf the beach we were on. "Oh, now, what are you bringing into your dream?" Triton said laughing. A loud roar came from the distance, and then we heard something big moving towards us. The water was slapping against the beach with power and force.

A giant figure started to come into sight and Triton had a look in his eye, like he knew what it was. "Are you guys ready to have a bit of fun?" Triton said with a smile that just cried smartass.

Nashani walked over and stood next to me. He was no longer an older man standing next to me. He looked to be sixty years younger. He had on what looked to be Native American warrior clothing. His body was covered in symbols and in his right hand he had a wooden spear with a stone tip on it. "What happened to you Nashani? How the hell did you become so damn young so fast?" I asked him.

"Nashani is not just a spirit guide like he likes to tell everyone. He is one of the great spiritual gods of the Apache people," Triton said.

I turned my gaze from Nashani to the giant one-eyed giant standing before us. I was not sure if it was real or if I created it in my mind. The giant stood over a hundred feet tall dragging a large club across the sand. "Um, Triton, is that a real Cyclopes?" I said to him.

"This is not real, none of this is. This is what Nashani calls a spirit walk - a way for a warrior to find his way once he has given up hope. Isn't that right, old friend?" Nashani just shook his head at Triton and got into an attack stance. I started to think about this all now. It started to make sense to me. I did give up. I did quit when Mira came to my house. I wanted to die, and I did not want to fight anymore.

The giant Cyclopes swung his giant club at us. As it hit us, it just passed through us like an illusion. I looked at Triton and he faded away and I found I was back in human form. I opened my eyes and I was back on the beach with Nashani, the old man was standing next to me. "So, boy, did you learn anything?" he asked me. I looked at him trying to see him as that young warrior from my dream.

"I did. I learned that you can never run from your destiny and that you have to stand up for those things you love the most," I replied. Nashani looked at me and then just like he showed up, he was gone like the wind. I stood there on the beach alone or so I thought. I turned to find Triton standing behind me.

"Well, I guess this means our dream roller-coaster is over, huh? Let me tell you your dreams are three ways to screwy. I have known some really crazy people in my times, but you take the cake, kid. But hey, I cannot say it was not fun, that is for sure. Now, go and save your love and kill that abomination they call the lord of vampires." Triton touched me on the shoulder and I could feel energy flowing into me. "What was that?" I asked Triton. He just smiled at me and walked back into the ocean.

I headed back to the diner and got into the rental car. I did not leave right away. I sat in the car looking at the blade. I could feel the magic radiating off the blade, it was powerful. I put the blade back into its sheath and set it on the passenger side of the car. I headed down to the ferry. It would arrive soon.

"So did you enjoy playing the searching game?"

I turned to see Teagan sitting in the passenger seat. He had the blade in his hands. I wanted to reach for it but I knew he would be gone.

"Teagan, why did you do it, why did you abandon the council? You know what the future holds if he is able to live," I said to him.

Teagan pulled the blade from its sheath running the pointed edge along his palm. "I gave the council two thousand years of my life. I turned my back on my own people to stay and help. I wanted more than anything to keep all of mankind safe. But I was wrong, mortals are nothing but blood stains on this great earth. Look what they are doing to her. Something needs to be done, and soon," he replied to me.

I could understand where he was coming from. But I knew that everyone should be given a chance to live and change. Teagan had it in his mind that no one is worthy of redemption.

"That may be true, but that is not fair. Why should everyone suffer? What about the newly born mortal babies? They should have a chance at life, don't you think so?" I said trying to reason with him.

Teagan looked out the window. "I am sorry, Liam, I truly am. I promise you I will do everything to keep Nyssa safe." With those last words he vanished.

I jumped out of the car not sure what to do. It seems like everything I try and do right, back fires on me. "Whoever you are that thinks this is a game, you are fucking wrong. I will not let you bring this world to its knees. I will go and find the vampire lord and I will kill him one way or another. Do you hear me?" I yelled to the heavens. I got back into the car and drove it onto the ferry as it docked. I started to think about what it was I needed to do first. Then it hit me. If the blacksmith can make one, why can't she make another? As soon as I hit the main shore, I went to the airport and got the first plane to Canada. I needed to find her, and, hopefully, she would make one more.

I landed in Ontario and rented another car. I drove nonstop until I reached that blue house. I got out of the car and went to the front door. I beat on the door like I was the police. Like last time the little old lady answered it. But I knew that she was also the blacksmith. "I cannot help you!" she said to me.

"Please if you do not help me, the world will be plunged into darkness and your kind will be hunted down. Trust me, the vampire lord will kill us all." She looked at me, no longer a little old lady but in her true form. This time she did not have on a mechanics jump suit but a long green dress.

"That blade was not easy to make. I had to bind it with my own magic. Inside that blade is a piece of me. I know of the vampire lords plans, but I do not think I have enough magic to make you a new one. But I might know a way; I will have to borrow some of

127

your wolf magic. If I can combine your magic with mine we might be able to create a new blade."

I looked at the blacksmith and I knew that I had to try. "I will do whatever I have to do to kill him. So if that means you need to syphon some of my own magic then let's do it."

She smiled at me and her dress shifted into the mechanics uniforms from last time. I followed her back to the room where she started to create the blade. It took hours, but I watched her work. It was amazing. She looked beautiful working, creating. The blade was done but it was not black like the first one. "So how does this magic thing work?" I asked her.

She walked over to me with the blade in her hand. "Touch it," she said.

I looked at her and then placed my hand onto the blade. As I did this, the blade started to become not black, but silver.

"There it is done," she said handing it to me. I looked at the work of art, its hilt was carved out of a tusk horn she had. The blade was silver and I was curious as to why it was not black. "So why is the blade a different color this time?"

She looked up at me. "Because it was formed with mixed magic. That means it can kill anything supernatural but it is also deadly to you. So be careful, if it is stabbed into your heart you will die, and so will your great creator, the Great Spirit. Oh, and I have one more parting gift for you." She walked over, kissed my cheek and I found myself back in Seattle. I was in the park near the docks.

128

Chapter XII: Knocking on the Devil's Door

I left the park and made my way to the Seattle packs warehouse/home. I needed to see if I still had the full support of the pack. It was not that long of a walk and when I got there, I found Giovanni's daughter coming out of the warehouse. "Hey you," I said to her.

She looked up at me and smiled. "Oh, hey, strange wolf. What brings you back to my dad's place?" she asked me.

"Just need someone to talk to," I replied. She smiled and then opened the door back up for me. "Have fun, my dad is not in a great mood."

I walked in to see the living room in a mess. It looked like a tornado had torn through this place. "Giovanni," I yelled.

"Yeah, I am here," he said picking his head up from behind the bar counter.

"What the hell happened here?" I asked him.

He looked at me and then looked around at the mess. "We had a bit of an uncontrolled werewolf issue. Our youngest member of the pack broke free from the backroom during the full moon. He tore through this place trying to get out of the warehouse. It is not a big deal, but he feels bad about it. I got a few members of the pack coming over to help clean." I felt him nudge me with the tip of an ice-cold beer. "Here, I am not drinking alone this early… that is for sure," he said with a slight laugh.

I took the beer from him, and then we went over and cleared up some spots to sit down. Giovanni took a few sip of his beer while looking around. "That boy is a wild one, I tell you. He has been hard to keep control of. I am thinking he might not be just a beta werewolf, but possibly an alpha."

I set my beer down on the only non-broken table in the area. "Giovanni, the time has come for us to take out the vampire lord," I said to him with a serious voice.

129

He looked at me with confusion in his eyes. "How are we going to do that? The word on the street is that you lost the only thing that can kill him."

I laughed and pulled out the newly created silver blade. "Let's just say I got a new one," I said with a big smile on my face.

Giovanni slapped my back causing me to knock over my beer. We both watched it fall and then we started to laugh. "What are you doing, spilling some for the homies?" Giovanni said, laughing.

I liked him. He was cool to hang with. I felt like I belonged here around him and his pack. "Well, Liam, I think that since you got the blade we can go get that bastard. I will call the other four packs and get them to come to Seattle today. What is the plan?"

I looked at Giovanni and I could see and feel the loyalty he had for me. I grabbed the beer off the floor and took it to the bar counter. I reached over and grabbed a rag to clean up the spilled beer. "I want all the packs in wolf form. Tonight is a full moon, so we will hit them hard and fast. Since Teagan took the last blade, they won't expect me to have you with me. I want you and me to stay in human form while the rest of the packs attack the mansion. This will cause confusion and give us a clear chance to kill the main targets. The vampire lord, his daughter, and that bastard Hannibal along with Dante. Yeah, Dante is with the vampires now."

Giovanni looked at me while I cleaned up the mess on the floor. "How do you know this?" he said with fear in his voice.

I looked at him. "Because Anoki showed me with his picture room. It is true - he has betrayed us, his brothers."

Giovanni got up and went to the bar counter. He pulled the phone over the counter and started to make some calls. From what I heard he was talking to the other alphas of the packs. After he hung up, he looked at me, his eyes golden with rage. "They will be here in two hours, and we will make all those vampires pay. I want you to allow me to be the one to end Dante's life, please," he said to me with a growl in his voice.

130

I looked at him and saw this news stung him harder than I had expected. "Why do you want to kill him?" I said to Giovanni.

"Because he is my mentor, my teacher. Him doing this stung me. I must be the one to end his life!" he replied.

I heard a knocking on the doors to the warehouse. Giovanni walked over and opened it up. I looked up, and it was none other than Dante himself. I jumped charging towards him. I was going to end him here and now. But Giovanni stopped me dead in my tracks.

"Let's let the traitor talk," he said.

I did not want to hear anything Dante had to say. I just wanted him dead. Because of him, everyone I loved was now a prisoner to the vampire lord.

"What do you want, Dante?" Giovanni said with anger in his voice. Dante looked at me and then back at Giovanni.

"Listen to me closely, my brothers. If you try anything tonight the vampire lord will not take it kindly. He has stated that you will either become personal wolfguards to his vampires or you will be killed. Do not be fools. Do what you think is going to be best. You can no longer kill him. The weapon has been taken from the so-called chosen one. Without it, you stand no chance at victory. I only come here to warn you because I do not want you to die on this night, Liam!" Dante turned and walked away leaving Giovanni and I.

Giovanni shut the door and turned to me. "I swear to you, on this night, his blood will flow." He pushed past me, and I could feel his wolf becoming active.

I did not say anything to him. I knew he would need some time to himself. Being an alpha means rage and power comes easier to us. So I knew time alone was what he needed to calm his wolf inside of him. I walked outside to get some fresh air. The sky was light blue, it was barely 10 am. I felt my stomach start to growl, I needed to eat. I walked up the dock to find a taco truck parked. I ordered four giant burritos and sat down at the tables outside the truck. It did not take me long to devour those four giant burritos. I sat there not moving right away, it was so peaceful and I have not had much of that lately. I looked over just watching the dockworkers lining up to get their lunches.

I started to wonder what it was like to have a regular mortal life, the daily routine of a job, a family and a home. All those things sounded perfect to me, something I would trade anything for. I felt the need to take care of all the wolves but I also wanted to leave it all behind.

"Did you save me any?"

I turned and saw Isabella sitting at the table. She had on a pink fluffy coat with pink pants on.

"Sorry, did not know you were going to pop in," I said with a laugh. She looked up at me shooting me an "I will kill you look". "So what brings my favorite fairy to see me?" I said smiling at her.

Isabella looked at me letting her beautiful dark brown eyes set on me. "I came to warn you that the vampire lord knows you will becoming tonight. I do not want to see you get hurt or even worse, die," she said to me.

"I promise you that tonight the only one who is going to die is him, and his entire coven," I said getting up and walking back to the pack's warehouse. I could hear Isabella running up behind me. I turned and she punched me in the arm and then vanished. *What is it with girls and hitting me?* I thought to myself.

I opened the warehouse door, finding Giovanni and Luther playing Modern Warfare on the Xbox 360. They both glanced at me, and then went back to the game. "So this is what an alpha and his beta does in their free time, huh?" I said smiling.

"You better effing believe it, my friend!" Luther said smashing the buttons on the controller. I walked back to the extra bedroom and decided to rest before tonight. I knew as long as Luther and Giovanni where there I would be safe. I climbed into the most comfortable bed I had ever been in. I closed my eyes and I was out. I awoke to the sound of someone crying.

132

I climbed out of the bed and entered into the living area. I could still see Giovanni and Luther playing the Xbox 360. But it was weird. Everything was black and white. "Hey, did you guys here that?" I asked them. But they did not move nor acknowledge me. I walked over standing in front of their game. Again they seemed to not see me standing there. I turned, again hearing the sound of crying. I walked out of the warehouse and I found myself back in my old house. I turned and I started to breathe harder when I saw a boy. He was not just any boy - he was me back when my father died.

I started to approach me, you could say. I was hiding underneath the desk in my father's office. I remember how much I hated everyone that day. They all came to show my father their respect. But in all truth they came to see what they could take of his. I looked at myself hiding underneath the desk and crying.

"I am sorry I left you so soon." I turned and there my father stood next to me. He was a spirit and he had no signs of burns on his spiritual body.

"DAD… is that really you?" I said looking at him.

He walked past me and kneeled down next to my younger self. I watched as he reached out and tried to comfort me. His hand passed through.

"See, your father did not abandon you. He stayed around watching out for you for a very long time." I looked over to find Anoki. He had on white overalls with paint all over them.

"I hate that anyone of you super powered supernatural beings can come and go as you please. What brings you to my dreams this time?" I asked him.

"I just wanted to say good luck tonight and I will do everything I can to help you. Anyway, get some sleep and I hope to see you tomorrow." Anoki hugged me in his huge arms and then vanished from my dream.

I awoke to someone shaking me to death. I opened my eyes to find Jenifer smiling down at me. "It is time for you to wake up and

133

come have some dinner." I looked over at the clock, and it read 6:00 PM. I was out for hours.

I followed Jenifer out to find Giovanni and Luther were surrounded by over fifty wolves. The living area was packed and they all were sitting around and eating.

"Oh, look who decided to wake up. I have gathered your army like you asked me to," Giovanni said to me.

I looked around more and I started to feel sick. Remorse started to come over me and I knew that some of these wolves, maybe even all of them would die. Is it really right of me to ask them to give their lives for me? I looked at Giovanni and I walked outside. I stopped at the edge of the docks and looked up at the moon as it started to peak out.

"What is wrong, Liam?" Giovanni asked me standing next to me.

"How can I be selfish and ask those men in there to give their lives for me? I am nobody to them. They only know me because of you."

Giovanni put his hand on my shoulder. "Listen to me, Liam. You are the chosen one - that means you are the rightful born leader of the werewolf nation. Every wolf here comes because of the loyalty bond they feel to you. What you are asking of them is not too much. Now get your head in the game. It's going to be a rough night, right?"

I looked over at Giovanni and knew he was right. I needed to suck it up and be the leader they needed me to be. We went back into the warehouse and found that the wolves were not human any more. Jenifer was petting one of the wolves; he was very big and had grey fur. Then I noticed the scent; it was Luther who was next to her. Giovanni looked at all the wolves, and I could hear him speaking.

"Listen closely, my brothers. Tonight will be a harsh and un-restful battle. I want you all to be careful and do not do anything stupid tonight. Remember that once the vampire lord dies, we will

134

be free from them once and for all." The wolves started to howl. The room echoed with their powerful tone. Giovanni looked at me and then back at the army of wolves. "Let's get it done, shall we?"

I opened the warehouse loading doors and the army of wolves passed by me with great speed. I watched them as they ran into the forest and disappeared into the night. "Listen, my little peanut, I promise you that I will come back to you tonight. But until then I have called you a taxi, and I need you to go to your mother's. When I am home, I will come for you. I promise you this." I watched Giovanni take his daughter into his muscular arms and hug her. He held her for a good while and then set her back down. "Let's go, Liam. I need to get back home to my little girl before the sun comes up."

I nodded, and Giovanni and I took off hitting the forest and running at full speed. We caught up to the rest of the wolves with ease. I ran side by side with Giovanni. It felt good once again running with another werewolf. The sound of the army of werewolves running was loud like war drums. You could hear the trees breaking and the ground groaning with them. We were less than two miles away. I looked at Giovanni, and he gave the order for the army to stop. Only Giovanni and I proceeded farther.

Because of wolf telepathy we could communicate to the army from over ten miles. Giovanni and I stopped on the cliff that over looked the vampire lord's estate. I could see Mira walking around in the hallway, and, next to her, she had Nyssa in shackles and chains. My wolf started to become enraged, for she had his mate and he wanted her back. I had to breathe slowly and keep him calm.

"Giovanni, I want you to hold on to the blade until I call for you. I am going to go down there and try to catch them off guard," I said to him, handing him the blade. He nodded, and I jumped off the cliff falling fifty feet and landing just fine. I walked slowly towards the mansion. I knew that they would soon sense me there. I found myself walking through the garden that the vampire lord calls one of his treasures.

"Well, I knew you would show up. You are so predictable!" I looked up the stairs, and saw Hannibal standing there. He had on all black and looked like one of those gothic rejects.

"So what, you think I would not come for Nyssa and my sister?" I yelled to him.

Hannibal laughed and then clapped his hands together. I soon found myself surrounded by five vampire guards. "The vampire lord wants to see you, Liam. Let us not keep him waiting shall we?" The guards grabbed me and pushed me along behind Hannibal. We entered the mansion, and I looked out the window. I could see Giovanni's eyes glowing.

Hannibal pushed open two giant white doors. Inside the room stood the vampire lord and Mira. I looked around, but Nyssa was not in sight. "Welcome back again, Liam. What do I owe the honor of your visit?" The vampire lord turned around. He had on a black tux, and Mira was dressed in a long purple gown.

"Let's see, I came here for your life. Would you like to give it up willingly?" I said with a smartass tone. The vampire lord laughed at me as he waved his hands for the guards to release me. Then he walked over to the glass case in the room running his hand across it. "Well, I would like to help you there. But it seems that you are short one thing. You no longer possess the blade that can end my life. So I guess I cannot grant your request."

Hannibal walked over and punched me in the stomach. I dropped to my knees because his blows were powerful.

"Oh, come now, my friend. Is that really necessary?" the vampire lord said to Hannibal. I looked up, and Hannibal just smiled, turned away and walked to stand next to Mira.

"Liam, I told you I gave you a chance to come back. This could have all been different if you would have heeded my words. Now I can no longer keep you safe. Oh well, I already have your replacement in place." I looked at her, and then it hit me. She was going to force Nyssa to be her new wolfguard.

136

I pulled myself back up from the floor. I could hear Giovanni talking to all the wolves. They were ready to kill all the vampires in this mansion. "I am going to give you one more chance. Give me your life freely, or I will have to take it by force!" I heard someone entering into the room. By the scent, I knew who it was.

I turned, and Dante stood there looking at me. "My great lord, Liam is not alone. He has an army of wolves hidden in the forest about two miles away. We need to leave this place before they hit us like a tidal wave."

The vampire lord started to laugh. "I will not flee from some dogs who got loose from their chains. No matter how many there are, they still cannot kill me. If you are scared, you may go, but I will be keeping your son as my pet."

I looked at Dante as he walked into the room, and then stood next to Hannibal. "Giovanni, get ready. They know about you and the wolves," I said to him with my mind. I looked around and noticed that Teagan was missing. "Hey, where is the traitor, Teagan?" I asked.

Hannibal looked at the vampire lord, and I could see fear on his face. "Well, Teagan, will not be joining us on this night. He had prior engagements, but I will tell him you said hi." the vampire lord replied. I felt two strong hands grab my arms. It was two of the vampire guards.

"Well, as much as I enjoyed talking to you, I think it is time we call this meeting to an end." The vampire lord walked over to me, ripping off my shirt. I stood there in just my pants and shoes. "Giovanni, it is time, give the order now...," I said to him.

The inside of the vampire lord's mansion started to shake. He turned and walked over to the windows. I looked also to find my army rushing towards the mansion. "I guess the meeting is going to have to be put on hold," I said laughing.

"Hannibal, get out there with the vampire guards and kill every last one of them!" he yelled. I broke free of the guards and ran out of the room, heading outside. Giovanni stopped next to me handing me the new blade. Hannibal stepped out and looked at us. I rushed him, plunging the blade deep into his heart. His eyes grew big with shock, and then his body started to burn.

I pulled the blade free and found that the entire security unit for the mansion was outside. I looked at Giovanni, and before we could rush into them, we felt great flows of air passing us. It was the werewolves, and they started to take out the guards. I rushed back into the house while Giovanni went in search of Dante. I made it back to the back room where I found the vampire lord standing waiting for me.

"What is that in your hands?" he asked me. I looked down and started to smile. "Oh, this old thing? Well, it is what I call the keeper of your life. With this, I am going to end you once and for all." The vampire lord hissed at me, and then the room went dark. I called upon my wolf, shifting just my face and hands. I could now see in the dark. I looked around but still lost the vampire lord. "Come out, you coward! I knew you would run!" I yelled into the darkness.

"Listen to me, boy, I am the first of my beautiful race. I am Vlad Tepes, lord of all vampires, and I would never run from a dog like you!" I felt a powerful blow hit me, causing me to fly across the room and smash into the wall.

I got up slowly. My body ached, but because I was shifted a bit, I did not get hurt too badly. I clinched my fist and realized that the blade was gone. I started to panic and needed to find the blade. "What is wrong, dog, lose something?" he said, laughing. I stopped and I could feel him. I turned to feel a sharp pain in my chest. I backed up slowly, the room lit back up, and I saw the blade, it was in my chest. The vampire lord walked over to me as I fell to my knees. Blood flowed out of me, making a puddle underneath me. "I told you that I would not die, and because you betrayed my daughter, I have decided to take your life.

I looked up at the vampire lord, staring at him in his blood red eyes. "I want to thank you for this night," I said to him smiling with blood in my mouth.

"What do you mean?" he said. With the last bit of energy, I moved to my feet pulling the blade out and plunging it into his black heart.

"I am thanking you because you missed my heart and gave me the chance to take your life." The vampire lord dropped down on his knees, looking up at me. I pulled the blade from his chest and stabbed him in both his eyes. I started to back up as a black energy started to shoot out of him through his eyes. Then his body began to shake violently.

"NO!" I turned to see Mira standing at the door.

She looked at me, her violet eyes shifted to red, and she rushed me. I turned, and Mira hit me, causing the blade to go into her heart. I caught her as she started to fall. She reached up with her hand and touched my face. "Liam, I am sorry for everything I have done to you. I just loved you so much. I would have done anything for you." I looked at her, trying to keep the tears back.

"I know, my lady, I know." I reached down and bit her on the side of her neck. I could feel it, the bond was gone, and I was me again. I left Mira's dead body next to her father's, and I took the pendant back from her. My sister shot out of it and looked at me.

"Liam, you came back for me..." I looked at her and just smiled.

I turned and left to find Nyssa. I took deep breaths, picking up her scent that led me to another room. I opened the door and found Nyssa chained to the wall, and standing by her was Kaliban. He looked at me with his dark eyes. Then something happened - the dark energy from the lord of vampires flowed into him. Kaliban started to glow, and then standing before me was a young red-skinned boy with long red hair. He was naked. "Kaliban," I said to him. He looked up at me, his eyes as black as coals.

I tried to approach him. He backed away, turned, and jumped through the window. I ran over, and he was gone, swallowed up by the darkness of the night. I turned and released Nyssa, taking her into my arms. "I love you so much," I said to her as she lifted her head and tears ran down her face.

139

"Liam, please do not ever leave me again," she said.

I nodded and embraced her with a kiss. I took Nyssa, putting my arm around her and guiding her out of the mansion. We stepped outside, and all I could see was a vast army of wolves. I started to become happier, as it seemed that not many died.

I looked over to my right and saw Giovanni walking over. "The night is ours, Liam. We have done it! We stopped the vampires from bringing the world to darkness."

I nodded to him. I was still shifted. I looked to the full moon and let out a loud howl. The rest of the wolves, including Nyssa and Giovanni, joined my howl.

Sarah Book Publishing

Also Proudly Offers These Titles

El Tigre II by John H. Manhold
The Phantom of Goliad by Dr. Herb Marlow
Sonuvacoach by Bruce 'Doc Leibs' Leibert
Jake Laughlin's Second Bath in the Same Year
by Cherokee Parks
Ben Solomon in Destiny Diverted
by Don Clifford
The Big Spin by Barney Vinson
Two Destitutes – Cold and Darkness
by Giorgio Germont
The Human Mold by Jose Antonio Jarimba
Hard Ride to Cora by Cherokee Parks
In Harm's Way by Dr. Herb Marlow
Journey of Faith "When the Path Divides"
by Dorothea and Fred Cole
The Tallith Ceremony by Rev. Lazaro Uribe
If Hope Is the Question... by Cherokee Parks
Obama: Out of Genesis
by Samuel Joseph Scott, Jr.
Buck Grayson – South Texas Freighter
by Cherokee Parks

Coming Soon

A Study of the Life of Christ
by Rev. Ralph Lawson, Retired
Remembering Sam by Jose Solis, Jr.
The Gift of You by Rev. Scott Brown
And MANY MORE!

www.sarahbookpublishing.com